My **ROAD TRIP** to the Pretty Girl Capital
of the World

Brian Yansky

# My **ROAD TRIP** to the Pretty Girl Capital of the World

Cricket Books
Chicago

No part of this publication may be reproduced in whole or in part, or stored
in a retrieval system, or transmitted in any form or by any means, elec-
tronic, mechanical, photocopying, recording, or otherwise, without the
written permission of the publisher. For information regarding permission,
write to Carus Publishing Company, 315 Fifth Street, Peru, Illinois 61354.

The Library of Congress Cataloging-in-Publication data for *My Road Trip to
the Pretty Girl Capital of the World* is available under LC Control Number
2003011594.

For my **FATHER AND MOTHER,**
William and Agnes Yansky

## **Exploding** Adopted Kids

The bell rang, but I stayed sitting on the steps by the cafeteria trying to decide if I was going to skip out again or go to English. Trinity walked right up and sat down next to me.

Two weeks and she hadn't said a word, and she sits down like nothing had happened.

"I know I've been a bitch. I'm sorry."

I shrugged. "Maybe we've both been a bitch."

I didn't have a clue what I meant. This happened to me a lot around her. Somewhere between my brain and my mouth, the words got all mixed up, and the wrong ones came out.

She paused but only for a second. That was Trinity. She'd let the little stuff go. It was one of the things I liked about her.

"I want us to be friends, Simon," she said.

Kiss-of-death word. Friends. How could it go from pie-in-the-sky love to friends in two short weeks?

I guess it was desperation that made me say it. "This is going to sound crazy, but what if we just took off together? What if we just got in the car and drove away?"

"You mean like a vacation or something?"

"No. Like going to the North Pole. Or like Stanley and Livingstone in Africa. A journey. Only we'd go to California. We could live on the beach. Learn to surf. Maybe sell exotic seashells for a few hours every day."

Exotic seashells? Mind-to-mouth problems again.

She stood. "I'm sorry, Simon."

"Not exotic seashells. But California. Sun and beach and stuff."

She took a breath, and I knew something terrible was going to come out of her mouth. "I'm with someone else now."

"Someone else?"

"I'm sorry."

I shook my head. "That's not possible."

What I meant was—not yet. I hadn't stopped thinking about her. How could she have not only stopped thinking about me but found someone else? There had to be a mistake. "I've been wanting to say something these past two weeks," I said. "About that night, I mean."

"I don't want to talk about it."

Our last night together she had told me a secret and asked me to tell her one. A secret for a secret. Why did my being adopted bother me so much? I couldn't answer when she asked.

That was it. The end. I became another on a long list of Trinity's ex-boyfriends.

"I know I should have said something. I understand. It's my fault. If you just—"

She looked away from me. "Forget it, Simon."

"I can't forget it. How can I forget it?"

She had a temper, and something I said raised it. She swung around like she was going to slap me. "I lied, okay? I lied."

"Okay?" I said. "No, it's not okay."

"You made me crazy always holding everything in. And I was mad at my father for leaving me and my mom for his twit coworker. I made that up about him getting into bed with me. It was stupid, I know."

I couldn't think of anything to say. Finally, I did. "You're right. You have been a bitch."

This didn't go over well. She stormed off without saying another word.

David Hooter just happened to come down the stairs then, and he did what he always does when he sees me. He made a lame explosion sound and moved his arms in a way that was supposed to resemble a mushroom cloud.

Normally I would have just ignored him, but Trinity had made me crazy. I reacted without thinking. I shoved him up against the lockers and then spun him around to the floor.

He had a surprised look on his face. I was pretty surprised myself. I probably would have got off him on my own, but before I could, Mr. Brown, history teacher and football coach and big admirer of David Hooter, his starting corner, pulled me off. He was not a big admirer of me.

He marched me down to the principal's office and put me in a chair in the outer room while he went to have a word with Principal Van Dyke.

I sat there thinking. First, I thought about how insane everything had become lately. With Trinity. With my parents.

At school. Then, when Mr. Brown still didn't come out, I thought back to that day when Todd Hooter, David's older brother, had told me I was adopted.

It was nine years ago. I was eight. I was playing air guitar with David Hooter over at his house. We got into an argument about whose sounded better. Then a wrestling match, which I was winning until Todd picked me up and held me in the air like he was trying to decide where to throw me.

I was a little scared because Todd could be pretty mean, but he just set me down. David got up and came at me, ready for a real fight now that his brother was there, but Todd shoved him back.

"You don't want to set him off."

David rubbed his shoulder. "What?"

"Make him explode."

David and I both stared at him like he was talking in another language.

"That's right," he said. "He's adopted. His parents aren't his parents."

"They are too," I said.

"Some of these adopted kids are put here by foreign governments, and when they turn eighteen, they're going to explode. He might be one of them."

David looked at me with new respect.

"Unless they get set off early," Todd said. He nodded knowingly at David, who took a step back.

"You liar!" I shouted and ran the two blocks to my house, thinking the whole way that I might go off any second. When I got home, I screamed at my mother, "Am I going to explode when I turn eighteen? Am I?"

"Going to explode?" she said, giving me her half smile, the one she always got when something confused her.

"Am I adopted, and am I going to explode when I'm eighteen?"

She told me not to move, which I took as confirmation of my condition; I began to cry. A few minutes later she came back with my dad and said that Todd had been lying about the explosion part but that I was, in fact, adopted.

"Are you sure I won't explode?"

"Of course not, dear," my mother said.

I wasn't convinced, but I decided I'd have ten years to figure out if they were lying. Then I remembered the other thing he'd said.

"You aren't my parents?"

"Of course we're your parents," my mother said, "but you have other parents, too."

"What other parents?"

"These other people couldn't keep you," my father said. "They couldn't, and we wanted you. That's all there is to it. You're lucky. You should consider yourself lucky."

And that was that. I tried to bring it up one other time, but my father didn't want to talk about it, and my mother got a hurt look on her face. It was like it was something shameful between us. I didn't bring it up again.

**M**r. Brown finally came out and held the door open for me. Mr. Van Dyke was sitting behind his big desk. He let out one of his nose-whistle sighs as I sat down. He looked more tired than angry.

"Here we are again," he said.

"I guess we are."

"What is it, Simon? What's going on with you? Trouble at home? What?"

The thing was, I did have trouble at home, but it wasn't something Mr. Van Dyke was going to understand. I mean, my dad had sort of come to believe I would disappoint him, and I'd come to believe in his belief. We argued all the time.

I got along pretty well with my mother, though she embarrassed me by reading these novels with disgusting covers (strong-chinned, heavily muscled men and beautiful, bosomy women locked in scandalous embraces). But the truth was, my mom was starting to look at me like my dad did, especially after last weekend when I got arrested for smoking pot out at the reservoir. A month earlier I'd been arrested for underage drinking.

I shrugged. "Teenage angst."

He frowned at me. Then we both sat back in our chairs. He stared out his window, and I stared at his pictures of boats on the ocean. I kind of liked them, even if they were a little corny.

"You ever wish you were there?" I pointed at my favorite one.

"All the time," he said, and then looked as if I'd tricked him. "But I have responsibilities. You should think a little more about that word. Where would we be if we all just did what we wanted?"

"Paradise?" I said.

He didn't crack a smile. "Out. Three-day suspension starting today. You get to come back after you, your parents, and I have a little talk."

I walked out of school down to my dad's old Chevy Impala, thinking about that talk. One word kept popping into my head. No.

I drove straight to Martin's mom's small, junky house and walked around back to the basement, where I saw Martin through the basement window sitting in his La-Z-Boy drinking a jumbo Dr Pepper. I knocked. He motioned for me to come in.

Martin was a big person. He weighed in the neighborhood of two-fifty and had a stomach that could keep him afloat on an angry sea. He had greasy, shoulder-length, blond hair, pimples up both cheeks, and bad teeth. He could look kind of frightening in a certain light. In another, he just looked like someone in need of a crash course in hygiene and nutrition.

Martin gave me his psycho-killer look, which actually seemed very realistic. "Where the hell you been?"

"Around."

"Around, huh? I got other people want to sell pot for me, Simon. You don't want to do it, then get the hell out. I ain't going to hold it for you anymore."

"You don't have to hold it for me," I said.

"I don't have to do jack for you."

"I know."

"You know? Shut up, you asshole. A pusher has to push. You ain't pushing hard enough."

In a weird way, Martin reminded me of my brother, George, who was in advertising and always talking about motivation and how to get ahead. My feeling was one way to improve the world would be to get rid of all the advertisers.

I sat down and watched some *Gilligan's Island* reruns with Martin. We talked a little. He didn't talk to me about my disappointing sales anymore at least. After a while, we just watched Gilligan screw up again so the castaways couldn't get off the island.

"I'll bet you five bucks the skipper hits him with his hat," I said.

"Shut up," Martin said.

It was a stupid show, but I was watching it pretty closely. That was how she sneaked up on me. Martin's creepy mother. She was ghostly white, thin as a pole, and had the same greasy blond hair as her son.

Martin glared at her. "I told you never to come down here."

Martin was giving her his evil look, but he was cross-eyed. Imagine a *High Plains Drifter* Clint Eastwood–type squint going off in two directions.

"Your father's at the door," she said.

"Not a penny."

"He's bad, Marty."

His father was a wino who didn't live at home anymore. He lived on the streets.

"You get the hell out of here." He struggled out of his La-Z-Boy. I was a little afraid for her, but she hurried up the stairs.

Martin went to a storeroom by the water heater and got me a kilo brick of Costa Rican wrapped in a grocery bag.

"I want to see your ass back here in three days with my money, Simon." His voice still had the same threat as when he spoke to his mother.

"Sure," I said.

"Don't 'sure' me. Just do it."

I drove home and locked the door to my room and got out my scale and Baggies and broke the pot into quarter pounds and a few ounces.

Then I went down to the basement where I knew my dad had cleverly hidden—if a thief happened to be visually impaired—his lockbox under the workbench. I picked the lock with one of my mom's bobby pins, just like I'd done when I'd first found it.

I pulled out my birth certificate and the sheet attached with the adoption agency stamp across the top. Two names, two addresses: Dean Dalton of Austin, Texas, and Kate Dalton of Dallas, Texas. I knew what it said, but I just had to see it again to make sure I hadn't dreamed it. I put it back in the box.

Up at school, I had my going-out-of-business sale. I slashed prices left and right. I was sold out in twenty minutes.

Then I got in the car, put it in drive, pressed down on the accelerator, and headed out of Mansfield, Iowa.

# Follow the **Yellow Brick** Road

It was between Aerosmith and Dylan's *Blood on the Tracks*. I put in the Dylan tape and turned south.

I remembered seeing Iowa from the sky when we flew out to Los Angeles once. It looked very organized. The roads seemed to form squares of different-colored land that made it look like a gigantic quilt. From the ground it was another story.

I got turned around a few times and recognized passing the same little town called Jollyville (nothing at all jolly about it that I could see) twice. I kept driving. After three hours I finally reached the border. A sign that was supposed to say LEAVING IOWA had the words GOOD RIDDANCE spray-painted across it. I took this kind of personally.

I was just starting to feel a little safer when the car engine sputtered and coughed, and then quit entirely as I pulled over to the side. I looked down at the gas gauge. Below E. A bunch of cows in a field stared as I got out of the car. They seemed to find me fascinating. I didn't feel the same about them.

I started walking. It was a pretty nice late afternoon for April. Not too cold, the sun peeking through the clouds every once in a while. Running out of gas was a bad sign. Not that I believed in omens, and I certainly didn't believe anything was happening to me because Jupiter was visiting Mars or whatever. But I didn't have a good feeling about the future.

I came to a small town that wasn't much of a town but had a gas station. As I walked down Main Street toward the station, a carful of guys passed in an old Ford so weighted down that the back scraped the pavement when it bounced over a pothole.

The car pulled into a parking space ahead of me. I kept walking and pretended to be very interested in my shoes, which were your basic Converse All Star Hi Tops. When I got close, I could see there were about ten guys packed into the car. How they all fit was one question. How they breathed was another.

"Hey," one of them said when I got close. "You want a ride?"

You know, my woodworking skills had never been all that hot. I once made a bat in shop that was thicker at the bottom than the top. His head was shaped like that bat.

"I'm just going up the block," I said, forcing a smile of general goodwill.

"Come on over here, man," Scary Head coaxed.

For some reason I remembered this fact from a psychology class: one in ten farm boys participates in some form of bestiality.

"I'm just heading to that gas station," I said, pointing like there were about a dozen gas stations in front of me and I wanted to make sure they knew which one.

"Maybe you are, and maybe you aren't."

One of the doors opened. A no-neck guy with thick, wide shoulders and arms as long as his legs got out.

"We asked you nice," he said.

I started hearing dueling banjos from that movie *Deliverance*. I mean, I really started hearing them. I thought that was very strange.

"Some other time," I said, like we'd be seeing a lot of each other in the future.

I was having one of those fight-or-flight dilemmas. It didn't last long. I was about to make a run for it when the big guy shrugged and said, "Well, if you're sure."

The breath I'd been holding came out in a cough. I felt a strange desire to laugh, which I realized could be misinterpreted by Mr. No-Neck as a challenge. I managed to keep myself quiet as they drove off down the street.

I looked around. Someone was watching me from the window of a nearby house. An old woman? She stepped out of view when she saw me looking at her.

I'm sort of slight. Tall but on the thin side. I've been told before that I have a young face, a kind of innocent face, which can be an asset when you get into trouble. One thing I'd never been told was that I looked tough. I toyed with the idea that my new independence set off an aura that had brought those boys to their senses. I dismissed this pretty fast and ran toward the gas station.

A piece of paper with the word CLOSED written in black Magic Marker was taped to the glass door of the little station. I could see a guy inside though, a fat guy wearing one of those blue shirts with his name (Dan) sewn on the pocket. He was watching *Dance Fever* on a TV with aluminum-foil rabbit ears. Some John Travolta wannabe was disco dancing up a sweat all by himself. I mean, the real thing was bad enough, but here was this guy doing it all by himself. "Stay in the light. Stay in the light." The fat guy watching the TV was singing. I wished he wouldn't.

I knocked on the glass.

"Closed," he mouthed and pointed at the sign.

I guess it was my recent proximity to bodily injury and the way the whole stupid day had gone that brought the tears. Just two, one out of each eye, but when I saw how quickly his face got sympathetic, I faked a few more and rubbed my right eye, trying to look pitiful.

"I ran out of gas a mile back," I said in a whiny voice. "And these guys threatened me—"

He opened the door, which wasn't even locked. I smelled the whiskey as soon as I stepped in. I saw a half-empty fifth of Jim Beam on the table.

"What guys?" he said suspiciously.

"Big ugly guys. The kind you see in movies who worship Satan and ride Harleys."

"The Duke boys," he said without hesitation.

I stopped faking the tears. "Who?"

"Brothers and cousins," he said. "They're a bad bunch."

The movie *Deliverance* must have still been on my mind

because I wondered if he meant that some were brothers, others cousins, or that they were all both brothers and cousins.

"I thought so," I said. "I thought they were going to kidnap me, but then they just all of a sudden took off."

He had picked up the bottle and was about to take a drink but stopped himself, holding it in the air. "Where did this happen?"

"Down the block," I said.

"Where down the block?"

"In front of that brick house."

Dan pulled a handkerchief out of his pocket with his free hand and blew his nose. If I was bleeding to death, I wouldn't have used that handkerchief. He took a drink from his bottle and set it back down.

"That explains it," he said, rubbing his eyebrows with his fingers, then brushing his cheek as if he thought something was stuck to it. His face kept getting more and more smudged.

"Explains what?"

"Why you aren't out in the country with the Duke boys right now."

"Because of a brick house?"

He took a drink of his whiskey and set the bottle down. "Because Bridget Bishop lives in that house."

"Never heard of her."

"She's said to be a witch. Famous around these parts."

"I saw an old lady in a window," I said.

"She must have given the boys the sign."

"What sign?"

"She moves her finger in a circle, and then a triangle.

Everyone knows it."

"Why would she do that for me?"

He shrugged. "No telling with her. She was nearly hung back in the fifties. There was a communist scare going on, and Mrs. Bishop was always having people in late at night to have their fortunes read, get potions and such, and the mayor got it in his head that a witch and a communist were pretty much the same thing.

"He was up for reelection and began talking tough about cracking down on a certain woman who the community had tolerated for too long. All of a sudden he started losing weight. Couldn't keep any food down."

Dan stopped to take a quick drink from the bottle and light a cigarette, a Lucky Strikes no filter. When he smiled, I saw a piece of tobacco stuck between his two front teeth.

"Then he got a cough. A couple of weeks passed like this, the mayor getting thinner and thinner and coughing more and more. Finally he announced that he had decided not to run again for mayor and he was real sorry for any slanderous thing he'd said in the past. Got his appetite back that night. Cough went away."

Of course I didn't exactly believe Dan. We're talking about a guy who couldn't keep his face clean. Still, those Duke boys had been scared off by something.

"I could pay you," I said. "If you could help me with the gas."

He eyed me skeptically, but I pulled out a twenty to show him I had cash.

He blew a smoke ring and stuck out a grimy hand. "I forgot my manners. Dan is my name."

I thought I should probably come up with an alias, but my mind went blank. He seemed a little put out by my hesitation. I panicked.

"Lassie," I said, and I shook that grimy hand like there was no hand in the world I would rather shake.

"Lassie?"

I nodded. My dog's name. She'd died four years ago, but before that we went everywhere together. She was my best friend.

"That don't sound like a name for a boy," Dan pointed out.

"It's a nickname," I said. "Just my friends call me that."

He ate this right up. His big smile, a missing tooth here and there, made his face look a little like a jack-o'-lantern.

"All right, Lassie," he said. "I'll take you to your car. Let me get my gas can."

He took my twenty even though I'd let him call me Lassie, but then gave me back eighteen. Just as we were about to leave, the phone rang. He picked it up. He frowned. "Is that so, John Casey? You're banning me, are you? What about the pissant?" He listened, and it was pretty clear he didn't like what he was hearing. "Pissant can't keep his wife from kissing me, I guess it ain't my fault." Pause. "You're warning me? You think what happened last night proved something? I was so drunk I couldn't even find my way to the rest room."

A deeper and deeper frown. "Oh, I remember, John. I remember *exactly* what happened."

He slammed the receiver down.

"You ready?" he said, as if he'd been waiting for me.

"I'm ready."

"I have to run an errand on the way."

"No problem."

We got in the tow truck. He jammed the key into the ignition. The engine sounded like a plane getting ready to take off.

"Better buckle up," he said as we pulled out of the drive.

Safety first, I thought, but felt less smug when he ran the only light in town, shifting quickly through the gears, the engine roaring. I fumbled for the seat belt and snapped it as we went through the big picture window of a small building with a blinking BAR sign over the door. Glass shattered, spilling all around me. I was thrown forward into the windshield and heard a loud cracking sound that for a moment I thought was my head.

Someone was screaming. Another voice, a man's, only a few feet to the right of me said, "Holy shit. What the hell was that?"

I could have answered that it was Dan, but I didn't.

A fog of dust floated in the air, making it hard to see. I smelled whiskey so strong it seemed like it was on my shirt. There were a lot of sounds muffled by the roar of the truck's engine: people moving around, things being knocked over, whispers.

"You okay, Lassie?" Dan said, breathing heavy, like he'd been running.

I felt my head. No blood. "I'm okay."

"Sit tight. I'll be right back."

He stepped out of the truck, reached behind the seat, and pulled out a shotgun. The sound of his pumping it caused a flutter in my stomach. He swung the gun so the butt rested against his shoulder and took aim at several targets around the room before pointing the gun straight up and shooting a hole in the ceiling. Pieces of it dropped and banged against the roof of the truck.

"Last night I was too drunk to defend myself when you assholes threw me out. Anyone want to try today?"

I didn't hear any volunteers. I looked over my shoulder and saw light coming in through the shattered window. A man jumped out of it and ran off down the street.

Dan fired the gun some more. Bottles and a mirror behind the bar shattered. More screaming.

"Goddamnit, Dan." I saw a head pop up from behind the bar. Then I saw the man reach for something, and the something was in his hand.

I opened my door and slid down onto my knees and crawled across broken glass and splinters of wood. I didn't know if the guy behind the bar had a gun or not, but the last place I wanted to be was in the middle of a shootout.

I bumped into other people on the floor, who were also crawling. I could hear a song on the jukebox, "Afternoon Delight."

"I hate that damn song," someone said.

Dan laughed. It was kind of a horsy laugh. The gun went off again, and pieces of the ceiling sprayed down like drops of rain.

I made it to the bar. I pressed my hand against its sticky side. I had a clear path to the door, and I took it. From somewhere to my left, I heard the same voice that had yelled at Dan yelling into a phone. "How do I know it's him? Let me see. His damn tow truck is parked inside my bar, and he's talking trash between rounds of gunshot. That good enough for you? Get your cowardly ass on over here, Tuck."

"Let's go, Lassie," I heard Dan shout from across the room.

The truck creaked as he jumped in.

"Lassie," he shouted. "Come on, boy."

I imagined people in the bar testifying at Dan's trial that he was crazy. Besides driving his truck into a bar and shooting holes in the ceiling, he'd been calling the name of a dog from a TV show.

I had nothing against Dan, but I had the feeling this was no time to be riding around with him. For all I knew, he might be planning to visit other people he didn't care for. I opened the bar door and took off running. Not that I had any idea where I was going. I cut down one alley and then another until I was almost back where I'd started.

I saw Dan's truck pull out of the bar, more glass breaking off the window as the truck bumped out into the street. I heard the jamming of the gears when he shifted from reverse to first. I knew I must be wrong, but I could have sworn he was singing, "Stay in the light. Stay in the light." The truck sped off down the street.

I ran in the opposite direction. Then I saw the witch's house, and maybe because she'd helped me before or because I at least knew who lived there, I ran up the steps and knocked on her door.

A police car, siren howling, roared by.

"What do you want?" a crabby old voice said.

"Mrs. Bishop," I said, "this is the kid you saved earlier. I need your help again."

Nothing happened for a long few seconds, and then the door creaked open. She wasn't as crabby-looking as her voice. She had straight, white hair that hung halfway down her back, and she was the ugliest woman I'd ever seen. At least that was my first impression.

"You better come in," she said.

I sort of hesitated.

"In or out." The old lady reminded me of my mom the way she said that.

I chose in.

"I'm having some tea. Would you like some?"

Tea was about the last thing I wanted to drink.

"Absolutely," I said. "Thanks for letting me in."

"I'm afraid Dan's going to prison. He's gone too far this time. Come on then, young man."

She led me back through several rooms. Though it was a big house with high ceilings, there was very little space because of the dense forest of things—furniture, books, newspapers, magazines, papers, knickknacks. We followed a narrow path that snaked through the rooms.

"My possessions are trying to push me out of my house." She smiled. It was a nice smile, and I thought I was wrong before: she wasn't ugly exactly.

The kitchen was the least-cluttered room I'd seen, though there were still piles here and there. Something was cooking on the stove in a big pot. She lifted the lid and dipped a wooden spoon in and sucked the broth from the spoon, a loud slurping sound.

"Brittle bones, bats' eyes, bakers' fingers," she said.

I was concerned. Yeah, you could say that. What if she had a monster son she called up from the basement using a whistle beyond the hearing range of the average boy? They would use my body parts for soup. It would be brittle bones, Simon eyes, Simon fingers. Not that I believed in witches. Witches were the kind of thing you really shouldn't believe in.

"Have you eaten?" she asked.

"Oh yeah," I said. "A lot."

"I don't mean in the past. Are you hungry now?"

"Full as I can be," I lied.

She slurped another spoonful of liquid from the pot. "Grandma's chicken soup."

It did smell like chicken soup, like really good chicken soup.

"Sit down. I won't poison you."

She made tea and served it with the soup.

"Saltines?" she said.

I was busy smelling the soup and looking for anything remotely resembling human flesh or bats' eyes. "No thanks."

At first I was just going to have a little taste and then pretend to be too full. Even though I couldn't see any thumbs or eyeballs floating around, I was worried. The trouble was, I'd never tasted better chicken soup, and after one spoonful I had another and another, and before long the bowl was empty.

"More?" she said.

"No thanks."

She got me another bowl like I'd said yes, and I ate all of that one, too.

"Those Duke boys weren't going to kill you," she said.

"They were just going to have some fun, but it's a bad kind of fun they were going to have."

"Yeah, well, I only stopped here because I ran out of gas. Dan was going to drive me out to my car, but I guess he's not going to be able to do that now."

"Doubtful," she said.

"Yeah. Well, he said you were a witch."

"Did he?"

"I don't believe in witches."

"That's your prerogative."

She picked up our bowls and took them over to the sink. A black cat wandered into the kitchen, and then another that looked like its twin.

"I don't have anything against witches," I admitted. "I just don't believe in them."

"I guess the Duke boys would say they don't believe in witches, either, but they sure jumped in that car fast enough when I made the sign in the window." She moved her finger in a circle, and then a triangle. She had a good laugh over that. She had one of those laughs that could sneak up the back of your neck.

She pulled a stool to the cupboard over the sink and got a round tin from a high shelf. It had a picture painted on the lid of two little kids walking in a forest and dropping bread-crumbs.

"Chocolate chip cookies," she said. "Your favorite."

They were my favorite. How did she know? I decided it was best not to eat any. But then again they were my favorite. I held out for a good thirty seconds before I took a bite. My head didn't do a three-sixty, and I didn't feel the least sick, so I ate nine more.

"Dan told me a story about you," I said. "He said you made the mayor of this town sick when he made things up about you."

"That was a weak and ambitious man in an evil time. Not too many people are evil, but a lot do evil things."

She didn't exactly sound like a witch. Not that I knew what a witch should sound like. Not that I believed in witches. One of the cats jumped up into her lap.

"Goodness, Virginia, you're a nuisance," she said, scratching the cat behind the ear.

"I mean, if there were witches," I said, kind of thinking out loud, "they wouldn't all be necessarily bad, right? People don't know everything."

"People know very little," she said. "Sometimes they learn a thing or two, though. You might learn something on your trip."

"Trip?"

"What would you call it?"

"A vacation," I lied.

She frowned at me. "I want to show you something."

She wasn't the fastest walker in the world, but I wasn't in any hurry to follow her, anyway. In fact, when she opened the door to the cellar, I considered taking off. But then I thought that she was just an old lady, not really a witch, and what could she do to me? *Just make me cough every second of every day and never be able to eat again was all.*

We went down steep stairs into the cellar. She paused at each step. The rough stone walls radiated damp and cold, almost like they were breathing on me. She picked up a twig broom at the bottom of the stairs and said, "I like the old-fashioned kind. They move better. You'll have to excuse the primitive nature of the place down here—no electricity."

She lit a candle in a holder attached to a wall. Then she lit another candle. This one she carried. I followed the light, which lit up her face, a mass of wrinkles and folds of skin.

"Here it is," she said.

Her voice stopped me cold. She held the flame close to something. I thought I saw a casket, but it was just the play of shadows on the shelf. She took down a gas can, and I could have just about kissed her. Just about.

It was dark outside when she drove me to my car in a black hearse, one of those old station wagon kind. She was so short she had to sit on a St. Louis phone book to see over the dash. I kind of liked her, and I wanted her to know it. That's why I said it. "I don't think you're a witch, but if you are, I think you're a good witch."

"I'm a witch all right," she said. "You probably notice a resemblance between me and Glinda."

"*The Wizard of Oz* witch?" I said.

"Exactly."

"Yeah," I said, which was a complete lie.

"Inside we are alike."

I nodded like I knew what she was talking about.

"I'm not just ugly because I'm old," she said. "I was always ugly. Ugly as sin my brother used to say. People just naturally thought I was a bad witch. I let them."

"I can see how that might be a good idea."

"There was only one man who ever loved me. He went off to war and didn't come back. The Germans killed him. But I've had a good life, and I've been able to scare a lot of people who deserved to be scared."

She laughed that laugh of hers. It was funny, but it didn't go up the back of my neck anymore. It was just a big laugh. I liked it.

We came to my dad's car, and I poured the gas from the gas can into the tank. I came around to the driver's side of the hearse. I started to thank her again, but she stopped me.

"Here's what you do," she said. "Follow the yellow brick road."

I don't know where the woman got her information. It was a little creepy.

She motioned for me to lean over, and I did. Sure enough, she gave me a wet one on my cheek.

"I hope you find what you're looking for, Simon."

She drove off. It wasn't until she was down the highway that I realized I'd never told her my name. If she was a witch, I guess I was just lucky she was a good one.

I got in the car, and I drove south toward Texas.

# The **King** of Rock-'n'-Roll

Just before midnight I ended up on I-35 south. I wished for about the tenth time I'd bought a map somewhere. I didn't know if I-35 went to Texas or not, but at least it went south.

By that time I was pretty tired, but there was no place to pull over, so I kept going. Once, I dozed off. The guy on the radio woke me by shouting it was one o'clock in the morning.

"Were you sleeping while you drove?" he shouted.

I was sleeping while I drove.

"You were, weren't you?"

He seemed to be speaking directly to me. I turned off the radio. I was a little frantic about it.

I got lucky about five miles down the road. A rest stop. There were three semis and a car parked in the little lot. I parked by a semi with New York plates and climbed into the backseat of my dad's Impala and closed my eyes.

Then I had trouble getting to sleep. I could sleep perfectly fine as long as I was driving, but settled and still, my eyes felt like they were propped open by toothpicks. Mostly I was just thinking how I'd finally done it. I'd finally done something so wrong I couldn't go back.

After a while I did fall asleep. I had a dream about a big storm in Mansfield and a funnel cloud that came right at me and lifted me off the ground. I was lost inside it, swirling around and around with cows and horses and especially pigs, there being eight pigs for every person in Iowa according to the almanac. But I didn't land in Oz. Instead I woke up just enough to roll over in the backseat of the Impala and remind myself I was parked at a rest stop somewhere in Missouri. That seemed a good long way from Oz. It seemed a good long way from everything.

The next time I woke, the sun was peeking over a hill like a one-eyed monster looking for a victim. I got out of the car and hopped around to warm up before walking over to the rest room.

When I swung open the door to the men's room, I had the sudden feeling I was a character in a *National Enquirer* story. While I wasn't in a Swiss chateau having tea with JFK or admiring Marilyn Monroe's calves at a rodeo in Texas, I was watching the King of Rock-'n'-Roll wash his tired face.

I admit I'd seen a lot of his movies, thanks to my mom, who dragged me to them when I was a kid. They were mostly awful. A guitar would come flying out of nowhere, and he'd catch it and break into a song. He'd gyrate all around while he was singing. It was embarrassing.

My mom thought he was wonderful. She had this Elvis Presley beach towel she would spread out on the sand at Lake Okoboji where we went on summer vacations. If you think lying next to her when she was on that towel reading one of her paperbacks with a busty blonde and a high-cheeked hunk on the cover was fun, you're wrong.

The guy who looked like Elvis splashed water on his face. He picked up a green towel draped over the edge of the sink and patted his face with it. I noticed gold letters on the towel—EAP.

"Come on in, son," he said. "I'm just about through. That road can wear you thin if you don't wash it off every once in a while. Ye-a-ah."

He looked like the old Elvis, the Las Vegas Elvis. Jet-black hair with those thick sideburns that food probably got stuck in all the time. Chubby, though his white jumpsuit with its wide collar and gold sparkles helped hide the fat a little. He smiled out of one side of his mouth like he had some special under-standing of a humorous aspect of life I hadn't caught onto yet.

"You got you a tongue, boy?"

"I'm not a boy," I said. Okay, maybe I was, but I sure didn't want someone like that calling me a boy and thinking he could get away with it.

"Down South we call young men boys," he said. "It don't mean nothin' negative."

I looked around, half expecting a guitar to come flying out from one of the stalls. Elvis would break into a song about how young men in the South were called boys just to make them feel good. If he started swinging those hips in front of the mirror, I was out of there.

"You're not Elvis Presley." I'm a skeptic, but I had to struggle with my imagination, which tended to undermine my skepticism in certain situations.

"Well, now that's debatable, son. The moon don't always rise in the same place, does it?"

He gave me that smile again. You had to wonder what was wrong with the other side of his face. He picked up his towel and told me to have a nice day and walked out the door.

I went over to a urinal, and after I was finished, I zipped up. It flushed itself. I jumped back. Then I looked around, but no one was there. I walked back over to it and stepped away, and it flushed again. Elvis Presley and urinals that flushed themselves.

I wasn't in Iowa anymore.

As I stepped from the rest room, I saw the Elvis guy pull out in a Bonneville convertible. If a car could stroll, that car was strolling. It strolled right past me. His license plate spelled ELVIS.

I don't know why I did it, but I followed the guy. I accidentally burned rubber pulling out of the rest stop.

The guy drove about fifty miles an hour, so I caught up to him pretty fast. There weren't many cars on the road, but a little pack had gathered around the Bonneville. A couple of women about my mother's age, in a powder-puff blue pickup truck, were shouting things at Elvis and weaving in and out of their lane.

Then something happened. One of the cars swerved to avoid the pickup and bumped another car that bumped another. I witnessed an illustration of cause and effect. Crunching metal. Breaking glass. It would have made Mr. White, my English teacher, my former English teacher now, I guess, happy as hell since he was always going on and on about the importance of cause and effect in essay writing.

I turned the steering wheel to avoid getting involved and just missed the car in front of me, but bounced off the road into the grassy ditch and up against a small, rotting fence post.

I slid out of the car into the knee-high grass. Several cars were piled up on the highway. The Elvismobile was in the middle of that pileup.

"He's gone!" a woman screamed.

It was one of the women who had been in the powder-puff blue truck.

"Son," a voice whispered. "Hey, son."

I looked down and saw Elvis on his hands and knees. He crawled into my car.

"What are you doing?" I said.

"Get in the car, son. We got to get out of here."

I didn't move. I wasn't taking orders from an Elvis impersonator.

"Please," he said.

I'm not exactly a sucker for the magic word, but it occurred to me that the police would be showing up pretty soon, and I didn't want to be there when they did. I got in the car.

"Drive, son," he said. "You get me out of this, and I'm gonna take you back to Graceland and buy you a new Cadillac. I'm noted for my kindness to strangers."

We bounced over the rocks in the ditch until we were beyond the cars. I steered back up onto the road and hit the gas.

The guy sat up in the seat and stuck out his hand. "Pleased to meet you. You can call me Elvis."

I frowned, but I shook his hand. It was soft and small, almost like a child's.

"What's your name?" he said.

My first inclination was to keep Lassie, but I didn't want to end up being called a dog's name all my life.

"Alan," I said.

It wasn't even a lie. I guess I'd left Simon behind in Mansfield. Alan was the name on that paper from the adoption agency.

"Pleased to make your acquaintance, Alan," he said.

# **One Fugitive** to Another

As we talked it slipped out that I was a fugitive from justice.

"Not that I did anything wrong exactly," I said. "I just left without telling anyone. And technically, I stole my dad's car. I'm telling you so you don't do anything to draw attention to us."

I realized as soon as I said this that it was a pretty ridiculous request.

"I'm sort of a fugitive myself," he said.

He pulled a comb out of his pocket and ran it through his greasy hair. I would have hated to be that comb. I could smell Brylcreem, which was my dad's choice of hair-styling stuff.

"If you're a fugitive," I said, "why are you driving a car with ELVIS license plates?"

His answer? He put on a pair of Ray-Bans.

I stuck a Jimi Hendrix tape in the tape deck and put on my mom's sunglasses, which were the only ones I could find when

I was leaving. They were kind of embarrassing because they had Garfield pictures on the corners of the frame, and the parts that curled around your ears looked like a cat's tail.

"You look like one of those Yankee grandmothers on a Florida beach," Elvis said, probably trying to get back at me for Jimi Hendrix, who was worth any number of Elvises in my opinion.

Anyway, here was this guy wearing a jumpsuit, sequins, and boots with zippers up the sides. It took guts to criticize anyone's fashion choice. Not that the glasses were my choice, anyway.

"So how come you were driving that car?"

"I picked it up in the Windy City," he said. "I couldn't resist."

The Windy City. I hated it when people called cities by nicknames. George liked to say he lived in the Windy City. When I thought about my brother, I realized my mother would call him as soon as she figured out I was gone.

Like he had sage advice to give. You know what he said once when I asked him if everything made him think of money? "Absolutely. The one with the most toys at the end wins, Simon." He may have sort of been joking, but only sort of.

Guys like George were always talking that way. Like it was an original thought. Like they were boldly going where no one had gone before. But even worse was when he started talking about how he was a street-smart shark. He was an advertising executive, for Christ's sake.

I knew George would tell my mom to call the police.

"Just call Chicago, Chicago, okay?" I said.

Elvis looked out the window. My dad had that same way of pouting.

"I better let you off," I said. "I don't need any trouble with the police."

I guess that was one of those self-evident statements. Who did?

"And here I was going to let you meet Priscilla and my baby girl, Lisa Marie. I was going to let you ride my horses at Graceland."

I wasn't exactly up on current events, but I hadn't been living on Mars or anything, either.

"You and your wife got a divorce, and your baby girl isn't a baby anymore. You aren't even alive."

Elvis took off his Ray-Bans. He gave me one of those bad actor stares he was so good at giving people in his horrible movies.

"Do I look dead to you?"

I didn't want to say what he looked like, so I said, "This is 1979."

"I know what year it is. Sometimes I just get confused on account of what happened to me when I worked for the FBI."

"Now you worked for the FBI?" I was beginning to worry a little. Why, exactly, had I let the guy ride with me?

"I know things have changed," he said, "but it's not right. None of it is right."

The way he was looking at me made me wish he'd put his Ray-Bans back on. I looked out into the day and away from those eyes. The sun was bright, pushing up into a blue sky; the road stretched out over small, rolling hills.

"You need to know the truth about me," he said.

"That's okay."

"No, you need to know. I'm going to tell you something I've never told anyone. I did some work for J. Edgar Hoover. He called me to do my duty for my country, and I answered. He sent me to South America, where a tribe had started worshiping me as a god. J. Edgar believed these tribesmen had certain extrasensory skills that could help America in international espionage and so on.

"The problem was, once these tribespeople got me, they wouldn't let me go. They took me deep into the Amazon. Meanwhile, Hoover died, and the actor he'd got to impersonate me was murdered. One of Hoover's associates must have got to him.

"By the time I escaped from the tribe and made it back to civilization, no one would believe I was who I said I was. In fact, they threw me in jail. Fortunately, I'd learned a few things in the Amazon, and I escaped. I believe there are agents out there still trying to find me because they think I'm a threat to national security and must be eliminated."

Generally speaking, I can always think of something to say, but I couldn't think of one thing to say to all of this. Finally, I cleared my throat and told him if he was such a big star, I guessed he could afford to buy some gas.

"I'd be happy to oblige you," he said, which counted for something since my funds were pretty limited.

I pulled off the interstate at the next exit and into a gas station. Elvis bought a tank of gas and two Cokes. He had a wad of bills in a money clip with a picture of Elvis playing guitar.

A baldheaded attendant and an old man wearing a straw hat eyed Elvis carefully.

The old man clicked his fingers like he'd made some extraordinary discovery, something along the lines of the origin of the universe.

"You're one of them Elvis impersonators, ain't you?" he said.

"I'm the real thing," Elvis said, but at least he didn't elaborate.

"I seen one of you in Las Vegas last year. That guy was something. Spittin' image. You could probably work on your looks a little and get you a job in Las Vegas just like that." He snapped his fingers again.

"I'm the real thing, sir. You just don't know the real thing when you see it."

The baldheaded attendant looked a little put out, but the other one said, "Like Coke. The real thing." They guffawed at one another. They seemed to think they were just about the wittiest gas station attendants this side of the Appalachians. I grabbed Elvis's arm. For a moment, I thought he was going to use some of those fighting skills he'd probably learned in the FBI, but he let me pull him out of that place.

About thirty miles down the road, Kansas City started to appear around us. Convenience stores, gas stations, motels, neighborhoods off in the distance.

I was kept pretty busy driving for a while. I'd never driven in a big city or even any city larger than Iowa City, Iowa. It was kind of shocking how people drove. A lot of them seemed to be trying to hit each other and me.

Then I saw a McDonald's with one of those signs telling how many billion hamburgers they had sold, and I jumped three lanes to get to an exit. I heard some honking, which people seemed to do a lot of in big-city driving. I honked back.

I was all set to get an Egg McMuffin when I saw another place just down the street that didn't even have one sign. I drove down to it just on principle, hoping they had breakfast. Anyone who didn't advertise always got my business.

Anyway, these chain fast-food places didn't serve real food. If you doubted that, just ask yourself one question: what chicken has fingers?

I parked and told Elvis I was going to get something to eat. Elvis sat very still.

"Sweet Jesus," he said. "I saw my life flash before me a dozen times back there, son."

I thought that was pretty amazing since he was supposed to be dead, anyway. "That was the first time I've ever driven in a big city."

"You're kidding."

"No, really. Could be genetic aptitude."

"I don't know about any of that," he said. "It may be your mama or daddy is responsible, though."

I didn't care for the sarcasm in his voice. We hadn't hit anyone. Maybe I'd grazed the guardrail as we came off the ramp.

"There's a gas station down the road if you want to get a tow truck," I said.

"Why would I want to do that?"

"Get your car."

"I was going to talk to you about that, man. I don't think I want that car no more. Fact is, if you'll have me, I'd like to ride with you. I'm going down to Dallas, Texas."

"How did you know I was going to Dallas?" I asked suspiciously.

"Didn't, but now that I know, I'll make a deal with you. I'll pay for gas, food, and lodging if you let me ride along. What do you say?"

He had his Ray-Bans off again. He was giving me his charming, boyish Elvis look. The thing was, he might really be crazy. What if he had multiple personalities? What if besides Elvis he became Attila the Hun or the Boston Strangler?

"Are you an Elvis impersonator like that old guy said?"

I was hoping he might come clean with me. Instead he looked hurt. "I'm no impersonator."

I thought about it a minute. I didn't have all that much money, and anyway, I was a little, I admit, lonely. I could always kick him out later.

"I'm a fugitive," I reminded him. "Just so you know."

"Right," he said. "You left without telling anyone."

"And I stole this car," I said.

"That ain't nothin'," he said. "I stole that car we left back there."

"But it had your name on the license plate." I realized I would sound crazy if someone was listening, but it was easier to go along with his story. Anyway, when I got stuck on a point, I had a tendency to forget the big picture.

"That's right," he said, "but it wasn't mine. I heard about this convention of Elvis impersonators, and I figured it was the perfect place for me to blend in. It gets mighty tiresome having to sneak around the way I do. But as soon as I walked into that convention center, I couldn't tolerate all those men walking around pretending to be me. I nicked the car. I felt like they owed me something."

I thought he was probably crazy. Still, sane people had made the world what it was today. That was kind of a sobering thought.

"You can ride along," I told Elvis.

He didn't want to eat, so I went in. They had what they called a country breakfast, which I ate sitting on a stool at the counter while I thought about calling my parents. I just wanted them to know I was okay. Also, I thought maybe I should tell them my leaving wasn't their fault. It was probably biological. I had a gene for messing up.

I got some dimes from a girl behind the counter. She was skinny and had a bad case of acne, but she smiled in a nice way when she gave me my dimes. I smiled back.

I got the operator, who told me to put my dimes in the slot. The phone rang. My mom answered, her voice sounding like it was perched on a broken tree branch.

"I'm okay, Mom," I said and hung up.

I went into the bathroom and splashed cold water on my face. I looked in the mirror, and it was like I saw a different person. At the same time I saw me, too. Christ, I was beginning to sound like Mark, a guy who had worked at the restaurant where I washed dishes last summer. He was twenty and claimed to be a Zen Buddhist. He kept trying to give me spiritual advice. He made a lot of statements about himself, too. *I am wise because I am not wise. I know the sound of one hand clapping because I do not listen when I hear. I see because I do not look. I find because I do not seek.*

The thing I noticed most about people who tried to give spiritual advice was that they were more screwed up than everyone else. Anyway, one thing was for sure. Nothing was going to be the same now that I'd left Iowa.

# We've Been **Expecting** You

When I walked out of the restaurant, Elvis was talking to a fat man with snowy white hair and a red face with a big nose. Another man stood near them, pretending not to listen. He was neat and compact and had mostly gray hair. His checkered suit looked as old and wrinkled as he was.

When I got to the car, Elvis said, "Alan, this here is Andy and Cookie."

Andy bowed and said, "Pleased to meet you."

He had a broad smile. His cheeks filled up like he had some nuts in there. We shook hands.

The other man nodded at me and gave me a tight little smile. I recognized that smile. He looked completely disgusted with the way things were going and with the world in general.

"I knew who he was right away," Andy said. "I read about people seeing him since he died. I told Cook all those people couldn't be wrong."

"And I told you," Cookie said, "that all those people are wrong all the time."

The little man wore black-framed glasses with thick lenses, but I could see his eyes clearly, and they were sharp as cut glass.

"Here is your living proof," Andy said.

Cookie looked Elvis over as if he were a picture he didn't particularly like. "He has done his best to resemble the star. Not too bad a job to the undiscerning eye, but an obvious fraud to someone like me."

"Forgive him," Andy said to Elvis like Elvis was Christ or something. Like they know not what they do, sweet Jesus.

"I've got to get going," I said as if I were on a tight schedule.

"Andy here was just asking me where we were headed," Elvis said, talking even more slowly than usual. You wondered, sometimes, how these Southerners ever finished a sentence. I remembered studying the Civil War and Mrs. French saying historians debated and debated why the South lost. Maybe they just overlooked the obvious: it had taken Southerners so long to communicate an order to attack or retreat that they were always moving in the wrong direction.

"We're headed to Texas, too," Andy said. "We'd sure appreciate a ride."

Andy gave me one of those pitiful looks dogs give when they want table scraps. To be honest, it kind of worked on me. I'd always had a soft spot for dogs. They were more reliable than people. They were always on your side.

"You don't have your own car?" I was stalling, trying to look them over.

"We're homeless," Andy said.

"We're bums," Cookie corrected. "I am a bum. No one wants to make distinctions anymore. I choose to lead the life I lead."

"I don't." Andy shook his head mournfully.

They were an odd couple. One thin and cold and one fat and warm as a Hallmark grandmother. I told them they could ride along. Anyway, if Elvis was a multiple personality, I would be safer if they were in the car.

"I'm thrilled to ride with the King of Rock-'n'-Roll and his good friend."

"You are too gullible for words, Andy," Cookie said.

I got us out of Kansas City and another fifty or so miles down the road before I pulled over and asked Elvis to drive. He'd sort of dozed off but pretended he hadn't.

"Right," he said. "I was just about to ask if you needed a little relief, son."

Andy got in front, and I sat in back with Cookie, stretching out as much as I could and closing my eyes. As I lay there, the tires humming, the air blowing over me like a steady warm wind, I started to imagine what my birth parents might look like. Was her skin color the same as mine? Was he tall like I was? Did he have wide shoulders? Was she pretty?

I'd had these dreams sometimes about being from this extraordinary family who, when they found me, would make me all the things I wanted to be. Usually they were foreigners, and they took me back to their land. Sometimes they were royalty, and I became this prince.

But this time I had a different dream. I walked up to a big mansion, sort of like Southfork on *Dallas*.

But J.R. didn't answer the door. This little guy named Hop Sing did, which might have been *Bonanza* intruding a little on *Dallas*. He said, "They've been expecting you."

He took me through these big rooms with books and paintings and posters on the walls. The posters said things like *Never Call Chicago the Windy City* and *Real People Don't Care to Know the Difference Between a Rolex and a Timex.*

In back, sitting by a pool, an interesting-looking guy in jeans and a T-shirt, no shoes, was talking on a phone. He hung up without saying good-bye when he saw me.

"What took you so long?" he said.

"I got lost."

"Glad you finally made it. I'm going to teach you to be all the things you aren't but want to be. But first we're going to have to talk to the lawyers about our numerous suits against these rotten advertising companies."

Then a woman who I somehow knew was my mother, I mean my birth mother, came walking out of the house carrying a copy of *War and Peace*. She dropped the book when she saw me.

"He's here," she said.

She looked pretty happy.

Then I glanced across the pool and saw my mother and father. My mom was crying. My dad was holding her and looking away from me.

## Running into the **Law**

I woke up in a sweat. I felt like Judas, Brutus, and Snidley Whiplash all rolled into one. What was wrong with me?

"I want to get back with my family," Andy said.

I looked out the window, trying to get my bearings. We were somewhere I'd never been before. That was all I knew. The sun was almost directly above us. Sometime around noon, I thought.

"How long have I been asleep?"

Elvis glanced over his shoulder at me. "Few hours, I guess. I'm afraid you made a wrong turn back there in Kansas City, son. I just saw a sign for St. Louis. I didn't realize the mistake until I saw it. We been going east instead of south."

"We've been going the wrong way all morning?"

"Close as we are to St. Louis, it don't make sense to turn around. We might as well go in and catch an interstate going south."

"I just want to get back to my family," Andy said again, more loudly, like he thought we hadn't heard him.

"Every bum says the same thing," Cookie said. "'I want to be off the street.' Not me. The streets are as good as anyplace in this inhospitable world."

"I got me a family, Cook. I ain't like you. Tell him, Elvis. We Southerners feel different about family."

"Don't bring that impostor into this." Cookie had one of those voices that made the person seem like he thought he was superior to just about everyone.

"I've had enough of you calling me a fake," Elvis said.

"Of course you're a fake. And as for you, Andy, this family of yours no longer exists. You're forcing me to be harsher than I want to be. Nevertheless, I can't allow you to wallow in your pitiful fantasy."

Andy's eyes watered. His face reddened. "You got no right, Cook."

"I can't believe no one noticed we were going the wrong way all morning," I said, but no one paid any attention to me. I was only the guy who provided the transportation. They were too wrapped up in their argument.

"Just don't call me an impostor," Elvis said.

A siren interrupted their scintillating conversation. It came from a highway patrol car on our tail, red light flashing. My first thought was my father had reported his car missing and now the police were going to arrest me.

"Damn, I was only going eighty," Elvis said, slapping the steering wheel. "Don't they got real criminals to arrest?"

He grumbled some more as he pulled over to the side of the road. The police car parked behind us.

"Will the driver of the vehicle please step out of the car?" There was some kind of speaker on the roof of the car that broadcast the cop's voice.

"I got a little problem with that," Elvis said, looking at me.

I turned to look out the rear window. I could barely see the cop in the car, but he looked scary. Mirror sunglasses. Crew cut. He looked like that cop in my favorite movie, *Cool Hand Luke*. "What problem? What do you mean you have a problem?"

"Expired license. Been meaning to renew it."

"Will the driver of the vehicle please step out of the car?" the voice repeated.

"You've got to go," I said. No Eyes. I thought that Paul Newman called him No Eyes.

"I sure don't want to sing no jailhouse rock."

"Your fans will demand your release," Cookie said.

Cookie's sarcasm set something off in Elvis. Just looking at his face, I could see something was going to happen. He shifted the Impala out of park, and the car shot backward.

We smashed hard into the front of the police car. Then our car, my car, or really my dad's car to be more accurate, shot forward about ten feet. Elvis hit the brake and backed us up again so that we crashed into the police car even harder.

Then we were moving forward again, the old engine roaring. Elvis must have had it floored.

I looked out the back window and saw steam rising from under the police car's hood. I also saw No Eyes jump out of the car and crouch. I heard shots.

Elvis took the first exit we came to.

"Anyone got a cigarette?" he asked.

"My dad's car," I said. For a moment I imagined trying to

explain to him how it had gotten smashed up. *Elvis Presley, sir, rammed it into a police car because he can't be taken in. FBI agents are looking for him. You see, this goes back to his getting sent on a mission to South America by J. Edgar Hoover.* I was dead meat. Then I remembered I'd probably never see my dad again. You'd think I'd be relieved, but I wasn't.

"Before I was a rock-'n'-roll star, I participated in a few demolition derbies," Elvis bragged.

"Now you've done it," Cookie said triumphantly. "We have to get out of this car, Andy."

"Elvis," Andy said, face white, his right hand rubbing his chin like he was wondering if he needed a shave, "sing us a little song, would you? Maybe calm things down. A slow one. 'Blue Hawaii' maybe."

"No cigarette, I guess," Elvis said. "Man, I would've loved to have seen that cop's face."

"I saw it," I said. "He's going to hunt us down and kill us all."

"Now, son, that's a tad dramatic, don't you think? We just busted up his car a little."

I was about to show him a little drama. Tell him to pull over and tell him he couldn't drive anymore because he didn't even have a valid license. But then I thought this was sort of silly. We were all going to jail for numerous other reasons if we got caught. Anyway, I didn't feel like driving just then; I was still feeling a little queasy about No Eyes.

Elvis drove down a little two-lane for about a half-hour, then made a turn onto a gravel road. "I think this will take us south."

Like the guy who'd just been driving the wrong way for however many hours was going to find back roads to Texas?

"I want a drink," Andy said. "How about 'Love Me Tender,' Elvis? Can you sing that one?"

"I don't feel much like singing, Andy." Elvis looked over his shoulder at Cookie. "Hey, you want off, little man, I'd be happy to let you off."

"We don't want off," Andy said.

Winter was still lingering back in Iowa, but it had lost its hold on the land we were driving through now. Leaves were beginning to dress the trees.

We left a trail of white dust behind us. After twenty or thirty minutes we came to a paved highway. I was glad to see it. Elvis stopped at the intersection.

"You gentlemen want off, here's a good place. You might get you a ride here."

"Better we take the long way and stay out of jail," Cookie said to Andy.

"I'm not getting out, Cook," Andy said. "I need a drink, and I want to ride along with Elvis and Alan."

"You're as crazy as they are, then."

"I'm not crazy," I said, beginning to really dislike this Cookie guy.

"You can always get out by yourself," Elvis said, looking at the old wino. "I won't miss you."

Cookie put his hand on Andy's shoulder. "We've been together fifteen years now, Andy. Haven't I kept us out of trouble? Haven't I always taken care of things?"

"You done your best, Cook, but I ain't running out on these boys now."

I thought, *Thank God we're saved.*

"We got to move," Elvis said. "We can't spend all day sitting here waiting for you two to make a decision."

"You been running things, Cook," Andy said. "I ain't saying you done a bad job, but I got to go to Texas. I got to see my family."

Cookie's face turned sort of strange. I'd seen that look before on my father's face when he went off fishing on his own because neither George nor I would go with him. It was a *to hell with you* kind of face, but now I saw something else, too. Maybe sadness and loneliness mixed with the anger. It made me feel funny to see it.

"Let's get out of here," I told Elvis.

Elvis hit the gas. The moment when Cookie could have opened his door and walked down the road passed. He pouted in silence. I hoped one thing. I hoped when I got to be an adult I didn't start this pouting nonsense. It made a man look pretty ridiculous.

It wasn't very long before we came to the Mississippi River.

"How'd that happen?" Elvis said. "Somehow we must have been heading southeast."

Somehow? Big surprise. We still weren't going in the right direction.

"That's Illinois over there," he said. "I guess we'll cross and then maybe circle back to I-55? I know that one. Heads south right down to Memphis. I believe we got us an interstate heading southwest in Memphis goes all the way to Dallas."

He looked at me. What could I do? I said okay.

We crossed the Mississippi, that fat snake of a river. I'd been over it before, but I never really paid attention. It was brown, slow moving, so wide it seemed almost impossible a bridge could go over it.

I don't know why exactly, but crossing that river made me feel lonesome. People had been crossing it forever, I guess. Maybe that was why. Or maybe it was the way the river seemed oblivious to everything but its own motion.

People were always talking about how humans had conquered this thing and that thing and how there was no part of the world left that humans hadn't conquered. But here was this big old river cutting right through the middle of America, and no one had conquered it. The fact was, it hadn't even noticed us.

# It's **Hard to Keep** a Giant Down

It wasn't long before Elvis said he felt plumb worn out and needed a rest. He didn't look too good. Maybe all those years in a South American jungle had caught up to him.

We switched places. Andy had been dozing but woke right up when I drove. Partly because when I pulled out, this car that could have quietly switched lanes instead tried to blast me off the road with its horn.

Andy decided he had to show me pictures of his children. I didn't have much choice because he stuck them right in front of my face. The boy was eight, and the girl was six. They were average-looking kids, but I said they looked interesting.

"It was a shame what I done to them," he said. "The way I drank. At first it was just a few beers after work. Then my leg, which I hurt in the war, started to pain me some. It had shrapnel in it. I started to drink a little more to make it feel better."

I rolled the window down farther. The warm air that came in made a soft roar.

"I sure could use a drink," Andy said. "Think we could stop at the next little town?"

I said I thought we could.

"Thank you," he said, gentlemanly-like.

I put in a Stones tape. Everyone got all upset and argumentative. Elvis said that wasn't real music. Cookie said if we didn't have classical, we ought to just have silence. Andy voted for Hank Williams. I reminded everyone we were in my car. Finally they agreed to let me listen to the Rolling Stones if I turned the tape deck down real low.

The problem was, it was so low Andy could still talk.

"Now, where was I?" he said, offering me a moment of hope he might have forgotten. "Oh yeah, my leg. When I came back to Austin after the war, I had me a limp. People would tell me about their war experiences, like to show me what a bad time they had, but they didn't have no limp. They didn't realize the difference. It pained me. The beer helped my leg feel better.

"Cold beer on a hot Texas day is a little heaven. I'd find me a nice little bar, a cool dark place, and drink after work. First I'd drink until supper, then it got so I drank past supper. Then I was leaving work early. Then I wasn't even going to work.

"My wife started nagging, of course. We got in fights. One night I pulled all the dishes out of the kitchen cupboards. My little boy came running into the room and started hitting my legs. 'Leave my mama alone,' he shouted at me.

"I couldn't stand it. I ran. I ran away. I keep planning to go back. Every day I plan to go back. I see myself walking in the house and her looking at me and saying, 'It's about time.'"

"Pipe dreams," Cookie shouted from the backseat.

Elvis coughed.

"It ain't no pipe dream," Andy said.

"You torture yourself. You should accept things the way they are."

"I'm gonna go back someday."

Andy sounded a little like the Cowardly Lion in *The Wizard of Oz*. He would have courage someday. They could have all played a role if you thought about it. Cookie could be the Tin Woodman in need of a heart. And Elvis could be the Scarecrow in need of a brain that worked right. I was thinking this was pretty funny until I thought about who that would make me.

"Dorothy," I groaned.

"What's that?" Andy said.

"Nothing."

I eased up on the gas when I saw a reduce speed sign. We came into a small town with one main street. I pulled into a parking spot at a corner store.

"Come on, Cook," Andy said. "I'm buying."

Cookie didn't look too impressed, but he followed us all into the store. It was a little past lunchtime, and I made Elvis buy us some hot dogs and chips. Neither Cookie nor Andy would eat anything.

Elvis and I took turns using the rest room after we'd finished the hot dogs. Then Elvis did stretching exercises in the parking lot. I thought about Andy becoming a homeless person. I remembered my dad and me down at the A&P one time a few years ago. We saw this old guy going through a Dumpster.

When we got in the car, my dad said, "He used to be the smartest kid in my class. Now look at him. A bum."

The guy was unshaven and dirty, and he scared me a little. "How did it happen?"

"He thought he was too smart for hard work," my dad said. "He was lazy and maybe a little weak. He let things slide. He didn't pay attention."

"I get you." The anger was like a sharp pain in my side.

"What?"

"I understand."

"I'm glad you do," he said.

**A** woman screamed. I looked up and saw a giant throwing her off the front porch of a small house right across the street. The giant had a face full of hair and was so big he seemed to be splitting his clothes like the Hulk did when he left being a man behind. The giant wasn't green, though.

"Now what do you say?" his voice boomed.

I saw Elvis race across the street as the giant waited for an answer. The giant had fists like sledgehammers and tattooed arms thick as tree limbs. I thought he would make hamburger meat of the face that had made a million women cry on the day of his death.

Elvis caught him off guard, though. He did one of those flying kicks Bruce Lee could do. Surprisingly, the giant fell. He rolled up onto his knees, bellowing like a bear. Elvis kicked him some more. Five or six times maybe. Very fast.

Elvis helped the woman up. Meanwhile, the giant got up, too. You couldn't keep a giant down apparently, even if you kicked him numerous times.

"You're a dead man," the giant shouted and ran into the house.

I started the car. Elvis and the woman ran for us, and I had to count one Mississippi, two Mississippi . . . to keep myself from hitting the gas. I got to six Mississippi before they jumped in.

I saw the giant as we screeched out onto the highway. He had a shotgun. I got us up to seventy pretty fast.

"Oh, Jesus," the woman said. "What have I done?"

I got the feeling it was a rhetorical question, but Elvis answered it anyway, "You got away from a man who was trying to kill you."

"He wouldn't have killed me, but he sure will now. Why did I do it? I just saw you, and all I could think was now's my chance to get away from Harley. Now's my chance."

The right side of her face was bruised, but I could see she was pretty and young, maybe only a few years older than me.

"Now, now," Andy said.

"For Christ's sake." Cookie pulled a white handkerchief out of his pocket and handed it to the woman.

"You're safe," Elvis said.

The woman blew her nose and looked out the window.

"His bike is broken. That's the only reason he ain't coming after us."

"Good thing for him he isn't," Elvis said.

The woman looked at him and sort of smiled a little.

"You look just like Elvis Presley," she said.

"At your service, ma'am."

"At my service?"

She looked around at the rest of us like she expected someone to explain the joke. When no one did, she began to cry again.

Cookie ordered Andy to hand her one of his tallboys. The girl opened it and took a long drink.

"Am I dead, then?"

"You're as alive as the rest of us," Elvis said.

This didn't seem to comfort her much.

"He's not Elvis Presley," Cookie said. "He's just someone who has taken it upon himself to try to look like the famous musician. I use that term loosely, mind you. His music is primitive and childish."

Elvis glared at Cookie. Cookie glared back. The girl looked around the car again. I could see her in my mirror. Whatever she was hoping to find, I didn't think she found it. She took another drink of beer.

"He'll come after me," she said. "He's probably over at John's getting some of his KKK friends right now."

I pressed down on the accelerator. "Your husband is in the Ku Klux Klan?"

"He ain't in it. Leastwise, he promised he wouldn't join. All his friends are, though, and he goes to their picnics and goes hunting and fishing with them."

"They have picnics?" I hated to think about what they did at picnics.

"Excuse me for saying so, ma'am, but you don't look like the type of woman to be with someone like that."

She blew her nose. "You really think you're Elvis?"

"Sure do, ma'am," he said.

"Call me Charley," she said. "I haven't thanked you properly for what you did. I sure do appreciate it. I never seen Harley taken down like that."

"Martial arts."

"It was a brave act. Harley was in one of his rages. Broke my arm last time."

"He didn't look like a nice man," Andy pronounced.

Andy drank his beer slowly, almost with a rhythm. It was kind of graceful the way he drank his beer.

"He ain't a nice man," she said. "He ain't a man at all."

After we went through introductions, the woman chattered about her life back in Troy. Her husband worked on a barge that carried freight up and down the Mississippi. Her town had a thousand people, but lost a few every day.

"Lost one today," I couldn't help saying.

She had never been farther than Memphis. Her family had died in a fire when she was ten. Mom, Dad, a baby brother. An uncle raised her. An evil man who lived on whiskey and pills. She married the giant to get away from the uncle.

We came to I-55.

"Should we go ahead and get back on the interstate?" I asked.

"We could maybe chance it," Elvis said.

"You all sound like you're wanted." Charley smiled. The smile held for a second and then went out like a match. "You are wanted?"

"Not exactly," Elvis said.

"Not exactly?"

Things got kind of quiet. I turned onto the entrance ramp to the interstate. Andy popped the top to another beer.

"I guess you're almost home, Elvis," he said.

# It's a **Good Idea** to Feed Them

I'd been driving for quite a while. I was sort of hypnotized by the road. The sound was like a shot. Then *clump, clump, clump.* I pulled over onto the shoulder and got the jack out of the trunk, but I didn't really know how it worked.

"Here." I handed it to Elvis.

"Should be easy enough," he said, then looked at the jack as if he weren't sure which part went under the car and which part went on the ground.

"I thought you were in the demolition derby," I said.

He claimed he had never had to change a tire. I said that seemed unlikely. We argued until Charley got out of the car.

"Harley could pick us off like ducks sitting on a pond here. You two watch out for him and let me do that."

Elvis tried to help her a little and didn't get in the way too much. I kept my eyes on the road and listened for the roar of

Harley-Davidsons. I thought back to a stupid movie I'd seen once where these bikers terrorized a family on vacation; I remembered a scene with the family cowering in their trailer and these bikers circling them and whooping like Indians in an old Western. Harley and his friends would be like those bikers. They would take our scalps to a KKK picnic and use them to decorate the tables.

"Could you guys hurry up," I said, which was my contribution to the process.

I noticed that Elvis put his hand on Charley's back as she got in the car. I put the jack in the trunk and got behind the wheel again and drove on. I'd never driven so much in my life.

"No one has told me where this car is going?" Charley looked around at each of us, like she'd just walked into a party and was asking where the host was.

"Jail," Cookie said. "The occupants of this car to be more exact. The car is probably going to be impounded—"

"Texas." I interrupted him, which was a little rude, but he would have gone on for a long time.

"I'm trying to get home," Andy said.

"That's nice. You been away long?"

"About twenty years."

Charley pushed back her straight, straw-colored hair. "Twenty years?" Then she smiled like she got the joke. "Where you all really from?"

Andy took this as an invitation to tell his story. He jumped right into it. Cookie let him go on for a few minutes before he said, "Would you please shut up."

"I'm just telling this young woman my story," Andy said.

"Your kids aren't even kids anymore. Your wife might be dead or remarried for all you know. You haven't even called or dropped them a card in all these years. It's a stale act, Andy. You want these people's pity."

"You got no heart," Andy said, taking a long drink of beer.

"Just accept what you are."

"Like you?"

"I'm a bum. When I wasn't a bum, I was a successful insurance salesman. Now I'm a successful bum."

"Cookie was a flier in the war. He's a college graduate," Andy said with some combination of resentment and pride.

"I don't regret becoming a bum. I hated life in the suburbs. I was a phony. At least now I'm not a phony."

Andy cleared his throat and looked like something was bothering his stomach. "You didn't just up and leave, either, Cook. You had your problems like the rest of us."

Cookie took a long drink from his wine bottle. "I didn't say I didn't. I just said I don't regret my becoming a bum. Sure, my wife and my good friend, my old war buddy Johnny Feldman, had an affair. I could have got her back, though. She said she'd come back."

His voice got louder and sharper. It was like a blade swinging in the air. "Like she would do her duty if I wanted. I told her to get the hell out. The truth is, I never belonged in that world, anyway. I belong right where I am."

We were all quiet after that. About thirty miles later, Memphis started coming up around us. I moved through traffic. I thought I did a pretty good job. I honked back at anyone who honked at me.

"Go into the city," Elvis said.

"Why?"

No one seemed to remember this was my car. The car kept filling up with people, and they all expected me to do what they said.

"I'm hungry," Charley said.

The way Charley said, "I'm hungry," reminded me of Trinity. When she was hungry, she expected to be fed. That was it. Life could become hell in a matter of seconds if she wasn't. I'm not saying I know a lot about girls. I'm no expert or anything. But in my experience when they're hungry, it's a good idea to feed them.

"Take the next exit," Elvis said. "We'll find a place to eat."

I pulled off the road and into the parking lot of a Denny's.

"I know a better place down the road," Elvis said.

He probably did, but I was tired of taking orders. I turned off the engine and put the key in my pocket.

"I'm going to eat dinner. You can wait for me or come in. Up to you." I got out of the car and marched into the restaurant. I flopped down in a booth.

I have to admit, I was sort of relieved to see Charley and Elvis walk in. They sat across from me.

"I'm starving," Charley said, "but I don't have a cent. I left my purse on the kitchen table."

"Allow me, then." Elvis practically bowed.

Before he even said a word, people were sneaking looks at us, or at least at him. Once he started talking, they didn't even try to pretend they weren't.

"You ought to wear less flashy clothes," I said.

Charley said she liked people who stood out, people who made other people look and wonder. Elvis just lit right up at that. I thought he was going to start kissing her right there in the Denny's.

"You live here, Elvis?" she said.

"Dallas."

"I've seen the show." She picked up a menu and lazily glanced at it.

"It ain't like that."

"Still, it's not the place I got in mind. I'm starting over, and the place has to be right. It has to be farther from Harley, for one thing."

"You're safe now," Elvis said.

The waitress came, and we ordered. Charley asked Elvis for cigarette money, which he handed over without hesitation, and she went to find a machine.

"I just love people who stand out," I said to Elvis, doing my best to imitate Charley's accent.

He frowned and shook his head.

"I just love sequins and boots with zippers."

I was just having a little fun. He completely ignored me.

Charley came back, already smoking a cigarette. She blew perfect smoke rings over the table. "I want to tell you something, Elvis. Harley wasn't always bad to me. Maybe I gave him some cause, too. It wasn't all his fault. Before I leave here, I'm going to call him, try to calm him down some, say goodbye and wish him a good life. Maybe he'll let me go."

"If you think you got to," Elvis said, obviously thinking she didn't.

We ate mostly in silence. After we finished and Charley smoked another cigarette, Elvis and I went outside, leaving her in the little lobby where the pay phone was.

Cookie and Andy were standing out by the car.

"You boys should have come in," Elvis said, but I could see he wasn't paying much attention to what he was saying.

"We walked over to that little store. Got a few refreshments and some beef jerky," Andy said.

Andy had bought another six-pack and some Boone's Farm for Cookie.

"You ought to eat," I said, surprising everyone, myself included. I sounded like my mother.

"To be honest," Andy said, "you lose your appetite when you're a drunk. At least when you're drinking. So, Elvis, you getting off here?"

"Dallas." Elvis kept sneaking looks at the door.

"You don't live here no more, then?" Andy said.

"I moved on."

Cookie had one of those fake smiles on his face, the kind some salesmen try to pass off. "Maybe we should drop by Graceland. You could show us around. Maybe hold a press conference."

"You're a man who don't believe in one single thing, Cookie," Elvis said. "I thank the good Lord I got faith in something."

"I been around fakes all my life. Give me an honest murderer over liars and fakes."

Every once in a while Cookie said something that sounded pretty reasonable.

Charley came out of the restaurant. Elvis let her get in first so she could sit in the front seat between him and me. She fumbled for a cigarette. Her hands were shaking.

Elvis pushed in the car lighter.

I backed out of the parking space. "What did he say?"

"He won't let me go."

The lighter popped out, the coils bright orange. Elvis put it to the end of her cigarette. "It ain't up to him."

She blew out a mouthful of smoke. I noticed her hand was still shaking. "He said he was going to find me. Harley always does what he says."

"How's he going to find you? We'll be in Texas by tomorrow."

"If he finds me, he'll kill me. Jesus, why did I do it? Harley won't never let me go. It was just—the way you appeared to help me. It was like in a story. Like a knight in one of those stories."

"Don't worry," Andy said. "People say all kinds of things right after a breakup. They don't mean them."

"You got away from him," Elvis said.

Charley silently smoked her cigarette down to the filter and then smashed it in the ashtray.

"I'm not sorry I left," she announced. "I'm not the least bit sorry."

I pushed in the Stones tape and got us on I-40, which would take us all the way to Dallas, Texas. Charley's leg sort of leaned against mine when she scooted down in the seat. Her sundress inched up high on her thighs. I tried not to think about her legs, which were, like Trinity's, the kind that once you started thinking about were hard to forget.

# I Might Sell **Seashells**

After I had driven us all the way into the night, Elvis offered to take over. I pulled onto the shoulder and got in the backseat. I had to elbow Andy a little to get him to move over. I could feel the tiredness of driving in my arms. I closed my eyes.

You know, it was funny, but what I missed was being home in my bed. Just lying there and thinking things over in a familiar, safe place. It was one of those things I'd taken for granted. I'd taken a lot of things for granted, I guess. Because I was thinking about home, I tried to think of a happy time there.

The one that came to mind was tobogganing in Whitman's cow pasture with my mom and dad. As usual, my dad insisted he steer because he didn't trust my mom or me. We went up to the top of this humongous hill. It had a sharp turn that had to be made or the toboggan would go straight into the woods.

Mr. Perfect made me push us off, and guess what? Right, he missed the turn. We went flying when the toboggan crashed into a tree. I loved that flying, that moment in the air when it seemed possible you might just keep going. I loved it even when I knew the landing might not be all that soft.

We spent the next few minutes brushing snow off our coats and pants. My mom gave my father a sharp look. My dad shook his head.

"I don't know what happened, Barb," he said.

He looked at the toboggan as if it had somehow betrayed him.

I thought it was pretty obvious, but I told him, anyway. "You drove us into a tree."

He glared at me, but then he smiled and the anger came apart, like a logjam suddenly cleared. He began to laugh. He didn't laugh that much, so his laughter took me by surprise. It was so big it filled the woods. It was so big you had to laugh along.

"All right," he said. "Let's try it again. This time we'll let Mr. Smart Ass drive."

I must have fallen asleep. When I woke up, we were under the white lights of a gas station, and Elvis was putting gas in the car. Charley came out of the store with a six-pack.

"I'll drive," I said.

When I drove from the gas station out to the interstate, I almost took the wrong entrance, the one that would have put me on the side heading back toward Memphis, but Charley stopped me.

"I'm still asleep," I explained.

I was just glad they didn't know about how I'd started out from Mansfield. People might start calling me Wrong Way. It was dark out on the interstate. The road closed up around the little light in front of me. I thought Elvis and Charley were holding hands.

"So why aren't you in school?" Charley asked me.

"I'm going to visit my father," I said, without really wanting to get into it. "Maybe my mother, too, but my father first."

"Where?"

"I don't know."

"You don't know where your daddy lives? He sounds like my daddy. No one ever knew where he was."

"I've never met my father before," I said.

It was quiet in the car before I said this, but somehow it got quieter. It wasn't like I really wanted to tell them about why I left, or why I was going to Texas, but I just started talking. It was dark and the car was small and the sound of the car moving on the road seemed to pull the words from me.

It was like I could say what I wanted, and it would be left in pieces along the road. It wasn't like telling a friend something; it was like whispering into the night and letting the wind scatter the words.

"I call him my father," I said. "I don't know what else to call him, I guess. I've never met him. I don't even know anything about him."

"He left you when you were young?" Elvis said.

"They both left."

That was going too far. I was sounding like I'd been abandoned on the side of the road.

"I was adopted," I said. "The people who raised me are my real parents."

I wasn't alone. I had parents. I tried to focus on their faces, but I couldn't clearly see them. I realized that the gulf that had separated us for several years had been so widened by recent events that they were no longer clearly mine, just as I was no longer clearly theirs.

"But I don't know," I said. "I was going kind of crazy in Iowa."

You don't know exactly when or how it happens. One day you're upset because you didn't get the bicycle you wanted, and the next day everything starts going wrong. For instance, your parents start saying these idiotic and embarrassing things in shopping malls and restaurants.

Then everything flies apart at speeds you can't measure, and a universe appears before you. Only it's not a pretty sight. In fact, you might like to go back to the time when your worries seemed immediate and focused, but you can't. What lies before you is so vast, so confusing, and finally so wrong that you hear yourself screaming inside. Meanwhile, the gym teacher tells you your hair is too long, and you tell him if you were him, you would worry about that shiny spot on the top of his head, and off to the principal's office you're sent for the third or fourth time that month. As you listen to the principal talk, you realize he is asleep, just talking in his sleep. You realize most people live this way. Sleep talking and sleepwalking their way through life.

But everyone looks at you like you're the one who's crazy and acting up and disturbing the peace. I knew I wasn't who I wanted to be, but at least I knew it. And if the only way the peace could exist was for the lies to keep going on and on, then that peace wasn't worth much. My parents never once asked me how I felt about being adopted.

"Everything is just so screwed up," I said. "I mean, how could I just go along with things the way they were?"

I waited for someone to stop me, but they hid in the darkness, and their voices hid in them. And so I continued . . .

"My dad just thinks I'm a fuckup. As soon as I started doing things different from the way he thought they should be done, that was it. I was screwing up. I was a great little kid, he liked to say, but that was a long time ago. He gave up on me. Washed his hands. And I thought, okay, I give up on you, too. And my mom is in the middle. She always has been, seems like."

Still silent.

I was a dog chasing my tail. I just couldn't quite get everything out so it was clear. "Anyway, I want to meet this other father and mother. Then I'll probably go out to California, someplace where it's warm all the time. I might sell seashells or something."

There were those seashells again. I honestly didn't know where they came from.

"You think he'll want to meet you?" Charley asked.

"I don't know."

"You should go home," Cookie said firmly. "Your hormones are out of control."

**71**

"The boy wants to meet his daddy and mama," Andy said. "He's got a right."

"He doesn't know what he wants. He knows what he doesn't want. He doesn't want to be like his parents. Every generation is the same. Did we want to be like our parents? Of course not. The difference is, we respected them. We didn't think they were corrupt. Since television, every generation believes the one before it destroyed the world. Television has made the young soft as cream puffs."

"And you're not?" I said.

"I gave up. It was a personal choice. You're a young man with your life before you. Don't try to fool yourself."

Like he wasn't fooling himself. Like he didn't wish his life had turned out differently. Anyway, who was fooling who? I might have asked my mom and dad that. I mean, why did they make it seem like a crime to mention anything to do with my birth parents? It wasn't my fault or their fault that there were these other people in our lives, but wouldn't it have been better to talk about them instead of pretending they never existed?

What the hell.

"You don't know what you're talking about," I said to Cookie.

Surprise of surprises, Cookie didn't have anything to say to that.

I drove for a couple of hours before I pulled over and let Elvis drive again. I sat in back with Andy and Cookie and drank a beer until I got sleepy.

I slept off and on. Once I half woke, and Charley and Elvis were making out in the front seat. Another time Andy was hacking. I didn't even feel like myself going down the highway in that carful of strangers. And at the same time I did. Nothing was clear to me anymore except that nothing was clear. I slipped back into sleep.

# **Elvis's** Birth Certificate

The air was almost light when I woke, the night still hanging on by its fingertips. I could see clouds covered the sky. I was sweating. The air felt thick. Andy snored next to me.

"Sounds like a buzz saw, don't he?" Elvis said.

"Where are we?"

"Big D."

We were not on the interstate any longer. We were in the city, or maybe a suburb. Malls and billboards and convenience stores surrounded us.

"You know where you are?" I said. I almost added, "And just call Dallas, Dallas," but I was sort of sleepy, and anyway, Elvis would probably start pouting or something.

"I live here," he said.

That wasn't exactly an answer, but I let it go.

Charley sat up. She had been asleep against the door. She yawned. She stretched. She had thin, fine arms. She was one of these girls who got better-looking the more you looked at her.

"Where are we?" she asked.

"Big D," Elvis said again.

It was too much. Hearing it twice like that.

"Just call Dallas, Dallas," I said.

Everyone ignored me.

"I'm hungry," Charley said.

Elvis looked pretty old in the morning light. Faded, I'd have to say. Grayish skin. Dark, swelling bags under his eyes. Lines on his forehead and around his mouth.

"I could eat something," I said.

Not that what I wanted mattered much. It was just my car. If Elvis was driving, Charley's wish was his command. All you had to do was look at him to see this was true.

About a mile down the road, Elvis pulled into the driveway of a restaurant and found a parking space near the door.

"Breakfast is on me," he said.

Andy said, "You're probably a millionaire a hundred times over."

We must have looked like a sorry tribe when we walked in, with the exception of Charley. I stopped at the rest room and splashed water on my face. When I came out, Charley was coming out of the women's.

"Seems like a dream," she said, "don't it?"

I had to admit it did.

A man walked past us and stared appreciatively at Charley. She didn't seem to mind. I looked at her smooth, long neck. I felt the sharp edge of wanting and looked away.

"You going on from here?" she asked.

"Depends." I didn't say on what, but I guess she probably knew.

She stared at me in a way that made me a little nervous. It was one of those invitation looks, except you weren't sure what you were being invited to.

"How about California?"

"I want to see California," I admitted. "The ocean, anyway."

I almost brought up the seashells again, but I caught myself.

"It's beautiful."

"You've been there?"

"No," she said, "I've seen it on TV like everyone else. Everything starts in California."

"That's what they say." I realized I had no idea who they were.

She touched my arm. Her hand was soft and dry, and my skin tingled where her hand touched it.

"I better go look in the phone book," I said. "See if his name is there."

It was pretty unlikely. Suddenly, the whole idea of finding Dean Dalton seemed stupid. After seventeen years I was just going to find his name in a phone book?

Her hand closed on my arm. "Harley wouldn't go to California. Least I don't think he would. He's worried about diseases, and he's got it in his head people in California got all kinds of diseases. I have to get away from him, Alan. I have to. If you help me, I'll be grateful."

Her face was close to mine. I didn't look away. I could feel her breath on my cheek.

"I'm probably going to California," I said.

"Think about it. Elvis might not make it, but you and I can. We could have a good time in California."

Her hand let go of my arm. She leaned forward, and her lips brushed my lips. I touched her waist, but she pulled back, and it was a good thing she did, because I was sort of losing track of where my hands went.

"Why wouldn't Elvis go?" I said, trying to get some control over this conversation. Anyway, I was feeling a little guilty.

"He says they have a group out there that spends its time looking for Elvis Presley."

"Do you think he's Elvis Presley?"

"'Course not. I don't think he thinks he's Elvis really. But I'm sure I ain't staying in Dallas, no matter what. If he wants to stay here, then he stays by himself."

"He thinks he's Elvis," I said.

"I used to dream of California. You think I'm going to make it to California?"

"I don't know."

"Wrong answer. You think about you and me crossing this country and what that Pacific Ocean will look like when we stand on the beach."

She walked away. I watched her for a second, and then I went over to the phone and looked Dean Dalton's name up in the Dallas phone book. There was a Sid Dalton, but no Dean and no Kate, either.

When I got back to the table, they all had their menus open. From a distance they looked like they might be in a traveling circus or carnival.

"Any luck?" Charley asked.

"No."

"Sorry to hear that," Elvis said.

No one seemed surprised. I got the feeling they had been talking about me.

"I'm going to Austin," I said. "I'm going to take you home, Andy."

For a second Andy looked puzzled, but then a marching band of a smile broke out on his face.

"I appreciate that, Alan," he said, looking around at everyone, lingering on Cookie, who was scowling. "I honestly do. You want to take me home, then by God, I'm going home."

When the food came, Cookie grumbled about cardboard toast and how the eggs had probably been poured out of a container.

"Nothing is real anymore," he said. "People have grown so soft they don't know real eggs from eggs that come out of a box."

"These are real eggs," Elvis said.

"You don't know the difference between yourself and a dead musician," Cookie said. "You certainly won't convince me you know a real egg from a synthetic one."

Elvis took a bite of his eggs like he was attacking them.

"These are real eggs," Elvis said, still chewing. "I grew up on a farm."

Cookie pretended to look surprised. He exaggerated the whole thing like a TV lawyer.

"If memory serves me right," Cookie said, as if there were no question about the service of his memory, "Elvis Presley didn't grow up on a farm."

"These are real eggs."

"All right. They're real. You know because you grew up on a farm. My guess is it would be a farm near where Elvis Presley grew up. But Elvis Presley didn't grow up on a farm."

"I grew up on a farm, so I guess Elvis grew up on a farm."

Charley looked intently at Elvis. It was as if she were measuring his nose, and its length was going to help her make a decision. She pushed her plate away and lit a cigarette.

"You've been foolin' with us, ain't you?" she said to him.

Elvis put his fork down. "No, I haven't."

"Shouldn't we be getting on?" Andy said.

Cookie had that fake salesman smile again. "What's the rush? We're learning something here. The truth. I'm a bum, but I don't like to pretend things are different from what they really are. In this way I'm an aristocrat of truth. I'm one of the select few who doesn't tell lies to himself. We've established that Elvis Presley did not grow up on a farm, and I believe this man when he says he did. Therefore, he is not Elvis Presley."

Elvis reached into his back pocket and pulled out his billfold. He opened it up and handed it to Charley. "What's it say? The driver's license."

"Elvis Aron Presley." She smiled at him and passed the billfold to me.

The picture was Elvis, a few years younger with a different haircut, but Elvis. I don't know why this made me happy, but it did.

"Anyone can have an ID made," Cookie said.

"Check inside the wallet. You'll find what you need."

Cookie pulled out several pieces of paper. He unfolded a white one. "This is criminal."

The birth certificate said the same thing as the license.

"Looks like you were wrong," Andy said.

"Don't be absurd. The dates are incorrect, and this man was born in Tennessee. I have a photographic memory, you know, and I am certain Elvis Presley was born in Mississippi. This man is the fake I've said he was from the beginning."

"You were wrong, Cook," Andy said. "This man is Elvis Presley. Says so on that birth certificate. You owe him an apology."

"I am a genius," Cookie declared, turning to me. "Surely even you people cannot be so out of touch with reality as to be unable to distinguish the difference between this man and Elvis Presley."

"He is Elvis Presley," I said. "He said he was Elvis, and he is."

Cookie got up and walked away from the table. Charley put her hand on Elvis's arm, and I felt a little jealous; after all, that hand had just been on my arm. He smiled at her and she smiled back, but something seemed wrong to me. His smile had no purpose other than the happiness that love can bring to a moment. Her smile was different. It had a plan behind it.

"I'm going to California, honey, with or without you," she said. "We'll go to Austin with the boys. Then we'll buy a car and go out to California."

Her blue eyes were steady. Maybe I was wrong about the plan. I certainly wasn't Doctor Love. What did I know?

"All right," Elvis said. "All right."

She kissed him furiously. "You need to get some stuff here?"

"Money," he said. "We'll need money. That's all."

He drove again because he knew where he was going. He drove into downtown and pulled into the drive-through of a bank. He told the teller to give him a withdrawal slip. I saw him fill in $10,000. The teller didn't seem particularly surprised. She asked him if he minded hundred dollar bills.

"I like them," he said.

She sent out the money. "Have a nice day, Mr. Presley."

The teller depressed me. Her automatic smile and the automatic words were just the kind of thing that I hated. And that made me pretty sure most people lived most of their lives without noticing a thing. She probably wouldn't have noticed if Marilyn Monroe and the two dead Kennedy brothers had driven up in a Swiss chateau.

# The **Pretty Girl** Capital of the World

We stopped for gas in Waco. Charley went to the rest room at the gas station and came back looking like she had met Dracula in a stall.

"You look like you're about to faint," Elvis said.

"I called him." She brushed back a strand of hair that had fallen into her face.

"Ah, honey, you ought not to have done that."

"I know. I know I shouldn't. I just keep thinking maybe I can make him understand."

Elvis shook his head. "A man like that won't never understand."

"I shouldn't have called. He's been drinking. He gets a whole lot worse when he's on a binge like this. He said he'll find me. He started guessing where I was. New Orleans first. Then Texas. He knew. Somehow, he knew."

"Texas is a big place," I said.

A lot of people said that about Texas. Also, if you ordered an iced tea, you should expect to get it in a glass big enough to drain a medium-sized pond. Still, not everything was big in Texas. The gas station attendant, for instance, couldn't have been much more than five feet tall.

"He's bluffing," Elvis said. "Did he know the city you're in?"

"I don't even know that."

"There, you see," Elvis said.

I drove out of Waco. It was a beautiful, sunny day now. It was like I was moving through the seasons. I'd started off in a coat, then switched to a sweatshirt and shirt underneath. Now I took off the sweatshirt. It was practically summer, probably almost eighty degrees. Back in Iowa, winter was just giving way to spring.

Andy started getting amazed when we got to the outskirts of Austin. He was an excitable guy the way it was, but the change in Austin really got to him. Twenty years changed a lot. Big surprise. It was to Andy.

What I thought was, if this is a big surprise to him, wait until he sees his kids.

At the 38th Street exit he told me to get off the interstate. We drove west on 38th past a golf course, where a pretty girl walked a golden retriever.

Seeing that dog made me think what I needed was a good dog. Maybe I'd be all right if I had one. But the problem was good dogs died.

I still remembered burying Lassie out in the country on my dad's friend's land and the funeral and how much it hurt.

George happened to be home from Chicago and came along, although he had to be his usual meddling self.

He told my dad he didn't think it was such a good idea to make all this fuss over a dog.

"What do you mean?" My dad always listened to George. He took anything he said seriously and considered it.

"A funeral and everything. Simon has trouble with his priorities the way it is."

George probably wouldn't mind attending a funeral for a Porsche or something. That was the kind of person he was.

"He loved that dog," my mother said. She was just about to cry. "We all did."

George and my dad exchanged looks. They could do that. They understood each other. They seemed to decide to drop it. Neither of them cared to face my mother's tears, I guess.

My dad was pretty good throughout that funeral until the end when he said he was going to get me another dog.

"I don't want another one." I might have been crying a little. I know it was hard to breathe. I know my mom put her arm around me. I think she may have been crying a little, too.

"You will," he said.

"You could get a new puppy," George said. Anything new always appealed to George. "Come on, Simon. A new, little puppy to take care of. You'd like that."

I don't know. I guess he was trying to be nice, but he just made me mad. "No, I won't. I never will."

Poor Lassie was barely in the ground, and my dad and George were acting like you could just replace one dog with another, like Lassie was a bike or something.

"Let's not talk about it now," my mom said.

My dad put his hand on my shoulder. "You don't know it yet, but you will want another dog. You'll love another dog, too."

I wouldn't listen, though. It would have been disloyal to Lassie. I still felt that way sometimes, but other times I wanted another dog. Other times I thought maybe my dad was right. I could love another dog, too.

"We should have exited south of the river," Andy said, suddenly, as if we were on a mission we would have to abort. "We lived south of the river."

"Driver," Cookie said, "stop at the first available place to buy a bottle. We're thirsty, aren't we, Andy?"

I didn't much care for this driver stuff. I ignored him.

Andy was shaking his head. "This doesn't look familiar. None of this looks familiar."

"What do you expect?" Cookie said with satisfaction.

"Dallas is the closest I've made it to Austin," Andy explained to us. "I've got to Dallas a couple of times, but I never made it down here to Austin."

I drove down 38th until Andy told me to turn left.

We passed a police car going in the opposite direction. I looked straight ahead, my palms feeling sweaty on the wheel. The cop was talking on his radio.

"Ordering donuts," I said, mad about the sweaty palms.

"This is a mistake. What can I say to her? You were right, Cook."

You got the feeling Cookie lived for those four words. He folded his arms over his chest.

We came to a big university. Stores lined the side of the street opposite the campus. Students crowded the sidewalks. You know, it didn't look much like the Texas I imagined. I only saw one person in boots and a hat, and not even one person had a gun holstered around his waist. The people were not rough frontier types. In fact, the girls were stylish and beautiful. Everywhere you looked, there were pretty girls. It was the pretty girl capital of the world.

"I don't know if I can do this," Andy said.

Elvis looked over his shoulder at Andy. "You'll be all right."

"We can get off right here," Cook said. "I see some bums out there. We can get off and get the lay of the land. You don't have to do this thing, Andy."

"I don't know, Cook."

"You want me to let you off, Andy?" I said.

"I better go with Cook. I better."

Andy made sure I didn't catch his eyes when I looked back at him. He looked down like he had something he wished he didn't on his shoes.

"Maybe you just need to have something to eat, get cleaned up?" I said.

He looked doubtful.

"We could get a motel room. Go to a restaurant. You'll feel better."

It seemed important to me, for reasons I couldn't explain, that Andy make it home.

"Maybe you're right, Alan," he said.

His hands shook. Sweat stains had spread out under his arms, as if he had sprung a leak or something. He had the look in his eye of an animal cornered and frantic about finding a way out.

Cookie saw it, too. He sat up in his seat and spoke loudly like he was defending Andy from the rest of us. "Andy doesn't need your advice. Let's get away from these people, Andy. It's time we got back to the life we are comfortable in."

"He just needs your advice," I said.

Cookie rolled down his window and spit out his contempt for me. He didn't get it all out, though. You could see that in his eyes.

"He wants Andy by his side," Charley said. "Like maybe he can't do anything without Andy watching and saying what a smart man Cookie is."

"The woman is insane," Cookie said.

"If there's anybody in here who's crazy, it's you," Elvis said.

"A runaway questions my motives, and someone who thinks he's Elvis Presley tells me I'm insane. Am I to take these criticisms seriously?"

I stopped at a red light. I had to.

"Andy?" Cookie said.

"I want to go get something to eat," Andy said.

"You just find us a Motel 6, Alan," Elvis ordered.

Charley looked disappointed by Elvis's lodging choice. Andy looked like someone who expected to be shot at any moment. Cookie pouted. You couldn't call our entry into Austin a celebration.

"Turn in here," Charley said.

I turned. Not because I was getting used to taking orders. I just wanted to get someplace and get out of the car.

"This isn't a Motel 6," Elvis said, like he thought maybe she was confused.

"Is that right, honey? If I had ten thousand dollars in my pocket, it would be a Hilton, but I know you like to keep your money as long as you can, so I'll accept this nice-looking motel."

The King sort of grumbled. You know, he was kind of hard to understand about half the time, anyway. In this case I understood that he was giving in. I parked in front of the lobby.

"Let's get us a room," Elvis said to me.

"Two rooms," Charley said.

Elvis frowned. If I were him, I would have preferred a room alone with Charley over one with all of us, and I was pretty sure he felt the same, but I guess he didn't care for taking orders, either.

As we stepped into the lobby it occurred to me that if I were going to put out an all-points bulletin for cop-car crashers, I would probably say something like an Elvis impersonator and a boy traveling together. I watched the desk clerk for signs of recognition, but she was a TV zombie. She had her little television on the shelf below the desk. Some talk show titled "Women Who Believe They Carry an Alien's Baby" was on. Someone who watched a show like that couldn't be expected to pay much attention to what went on outside the confines of the TV screen.

She handed Elvis the key.

"Can you believe this?" she said. "Women who think an alien has made them pregnant?"

Elvis was about to answer, but I pulled him away.

"Why did you do that?" he said as we walked out.

"Do what?"

"You got to have better manners than that, Alan. That girl asked me a question."

"I didn't want to keep everyone waiting," I said, which we both knew was a little out of character.

He looked hurt. He sort of had these puppy dog eyes, anyway. He picked up his pace and got ahead of me. I had to run to catch up, which didn't make me all that happy.

"Okay," I said.

"Okay what?" he said.

You would think a guy like that wouldn't notice much, but people surprised you sometimes. "Okay, I'm sorry."

"Don't worry about it, son," he said, brightening right up. "You got to trust me. I know for a fact aliens don't care to mate with earthwomen."

I could have sworn I saw a slight smile, and not that usual lopsided grin, either.

## 21 **Rambling** Rose

Andy was in the bathroom for a long time. When we started to hear Elvis and Charley fooling around through the paper-thin walls, Cookie said he was going out to get something to drink.

Before he left, he said, "If you wonder why all the great thinkers have said man will destroy himself, just take a look around you. You've got an old fool getting all prettied up for a family that has long forgotten him. And you have a middle-aged madman enjoying the fruits of a runaway wife solely because he has ten thousand dollars."

I wasn't all that broken up about Cookie leaving, though his slamming the door on the way out pretty much proved he wasn't all that superior. I turned on the TV and flipped through the stations.

The news was on. I didn't care much for the news, but I watched it anyway. There was the usual stuff about the economy not doing so well.

There was some senator promising that sooner or later we were going to have to fight the Russians. We better be ready.

Like everyone didn't know the world was going to end if the Soviet Union and the United States started using all those missiles and bombs they had pointed at each other. Like we were completely stupid. Some days, I'll be honest, I didn't think it would be such a bad thing to have a nuclear war. Maybe humans could do a better job next time.

After the senator, a newscaster interviewed this guy who was making computers, who said, "Computers will save the economy. People don't realize it yet, but the world is changing. Computers are the future. They're cool."

He was kind of nerdy-looking, but you had to admire his passion.

The announcers back at the Channel 7 newsroom were smirking. They looked almost alike, these newscasters. Both of them looked like Barbie's boyfriend, Ken. That hair. That smile.

"The word *cool* went out with the sixties," one of them said. "Someone should have told him."

Then the other announcer said, "Computers, huh? In spite of that *cool* guy's advice, I wouldn't recommend you folks out there rush off and invest in computers. Personally, I think I'll just keep my money in oil companies."

They had a good laugh. They acted like they were witty as could be. I felt like throwing up watching those two.

Andy came out of the bathroom, hair slicked back, skin looking a shade lighter without the dirt.

"I could use a suit," he said. "These clothes ain't much."

I told him he looked all right, but those clothes had grease marks and stains that were like a map of his failure. I could understand his wanting to get rid of them.

"Used to be there was this secondhand store on Congress. Not too far from here."

He kind of looked away when he said this, but I already knew I was going to take him. I wanted to get out of that room, anyway.

"Okay, Andy," I said. "Let's go."

He smiled that broken old smile of his. For just a moment he reminded me of Lassie in Lassie's old days. Teeth broken off and yellowed from chewing rocks and not brushing regularly or, actually, at all.

I drove Andy down to the secondhand store, which amazingly was still there. He bought a pretty awful checkered suit that looked like it was made for a used-car salesman.

"How do I look?"

"Great," I said.

When we got back to the motel, Cookie was waiting in the room and in a pretty bad mood, even though he had a bottle of wine in his hand. A six-pack of beer sat on the dresser.

"You look ridiculous," he said to Andy right off.

Charley and Elvis showed up about this time. Charley made a big fuss over Andy to offset Cookie's criticism.

"I could eat a horse," Elvis said.

People who said stuff like that made me wish I had a horse handy.

Even though it was my car, Elvis had to drive. Charley sat in the seat between us. She pushed back her hair, which was damp from a shower and smelled like the air when the rain had washed it clean.

The restaurant he chose to stop at was called King Chicken.

"The irony. The irony," Cookie said, sounding a little drunk.

The waiter who greeted us when we came in said, "Whoa," to Elvis. "How's the Colonel? How's the hound dog? I'm having an Elvis sighting. I can't believe it. Either that or a nervous breakdown."

Elvis wasn't amused. A lot of people in the restaurant were. They watched Elvis follow the waiter. It was kind of strange. They were laughing, but they were also nervous. They were hoping, I thought, that something would happen that would prove this wasn't all just a joke. I realized people still wanted something from Elvis.

The five of us sat at a round table toward the back.

"Your Highness? Jack Daniel's?" the waiter said.

Elvis cut the guy in two with a look. I sympathized, but I had to admit he sort of asked for it.

"Iced tea," Elvis said.

"And your son and daughter?" He was a bitchy little waiter.

"You better keep your day job," Charley said. "You ain't never going to make it as a comic."

I laughed. That was my contribution. From the looks of the guy, we weren't going to be eating anytime soon.

I got up and did what I'd been putting off doing since we arrived in Austin. I walked back to the phone and lifted the phone book attached to the chain and opened it up to the Ds.

I got to Dalquist and stopped. I could feel my heart trying to break out of my body.

I forced my finger down the page. It rested right beneath one name: Dean Dalton, 21 Rambling Rose. No Kate Dalton, which wasn't really a surprise. The surprise was Dean's name. I coughed as I tore the page out of the phone book.

When I got back to the table, I saw that things had deteriorated in my absence. Andy was paying close attention to his drink. Cookie was staring at the table like he was involved in a chess game and trying to decide his next move. Elvis and Charley were in the middle of a fight.

"They knew you at that bank," she said. "They knew you real good."

"So?"

"So maybe I find it hard to believe you just got that ten thousand dollars. It's a matter of trust, Elvis."

Charley pushed her chair back from the table and lit a cigarette.

"I had a lot of money once, Charley. I had it, and I lost it. When I came back from South America, it wasn't easy for me."

"How did you lose it?"

"Gambling."

Charley blew smoke out in a cloud over the table. "You were one of those Elvis impersonators out in Las Vegas, weren't you?"

She was looking smart and cool as the North Pole. Elvis got up; he walked right out of the restaurant.

Charley stubbed out her cigarette. "What's with him?"

She still thought that Elvis was performing or playing some kind of game. We all sat there, kind of quiet for a few seconds, and then she said, "He walks out on me again, he better keep walking." She practically knocked over her chair when she left.

Andy leaned toward me and whispered, like it was a secret, "Your daddy here, Alan?"

"Why in the world," Cookie said, "would a grown man call his father Daddy? I simply cannot understand this Southern tradition."

For once I had to agree with Cookie.

"He's here," I said.

They both looked surprised.

"Congratulations," Cookie said, and he seemed almost human.

"Your daddy is going to be one surprised man," Andy said.

I thought that was a pretty safe statement.

Charley came back and sat down. The waiter finally brought our food, but Charley didn't eat any. She lit a cigarette. You could tell this pissed off Cookie. She didn't seem to mind.

"He's asleep in the backseat," she said finally. "I could hardly wake him, and when I did, he talked all crazy."

"Is he all right?"

She shrugged. "I don't know. He went ballistic on me. He started talking about J. Edgar Hoover and South America."

"I know about it," I said. "He told me that story."

"He believes it?"

It was my turn to shrug.

"Oh no," she said. "He really thinks he's Elvis Presley? He really does?"

Cookie said she was finally getting it. I didn't say anything. Even Andy didn't say anything.

Charley let those pretty blue eyes rest right on mine. She was the kind of girl who could inspire the imagination. "I got to have someone I can depend on. How about you, Alan? You gonna go with us to California?"

"He's here," I said. "My dad. His name's in the phone book, anyway."

She smiled, but it wasn't a happy smile. Still, she touched my arm and said, "Good for you. Good for you, hon."

She paid the bill with some of Elvis's money, and we walked out. The car trip had held us together, but now that we were in Austin, we were coming apart. I hadn't really thought much about it, but (I know this will sound crazy) I'd kind of got used to us all being together. Almost like we were a family.

Elvis woke up a little when we got to the car. His eyes were puffy, and the lines on his face were like one of those maps that shows all the rivers and mountains and stuff. He looked about a hundred years old. Charley and I got in front. Andy and Cookie got in back.

"Elvis," Andy said, "you just rest now."

Oddest thing, Elvis lay his head on Andy's shoulder, closed his eyes, and went right to sleep.

# She Was **Looking at Me** Like I Was Already in the Past

When we got back to the motel, I woke Elvis. Charley didn't say a word, but she seemed different. I couldn't say how exactly. It was the way she looked at all of us.

"Never sleep more than three or four hours a night," Elvis said as I helped him up to his room. He was leaning heavily against me like he was drunk or something.

The moment we got inside, he took three long steps to the bed and fell on it. He went right back to sleep.

"You think he'll be all right?" I said.

Charley sat in the chair beside the bed. "I don't know a thing about it really. I thought he—I thought he was something he isn't."

"He'll be all right," I said, but I wasn't so sure.

"I don't know about that. Anyway, what about me? Am I going to be all right?"

When she saw I didn't have an answer, she told me to get out.

As I closed the door she looked up at me with a certain expression I'd seen on Trinity's face before she dumped me. She saw the future, or she saw her future, anyway. She was looking over her shoulder at me like I was already in the past. It didn't make me feel good to see Charley look at me like that, but it made me feel worse to see her look at Elvis that way.

Cookie and Andy were waiting in the hall because I had the key. I opened the door and pretended to be a suave gentleman, swinging my arm to motion Cookie and Andy in before me. Andy was gracious enough to walk in, but Cookie looked like he was about to lecture me on horseplay. He settled for a derisive snort.

Andy turned on the TV first thing and started switching channels. He giggled at stupid commercials. He especially loved that Charmin commercial with Mr. Whipple. He was not a quiet TV watcher.

"You are worse than a child when you get around a television," Cookie said.

"It ain't a crime to like TV, is it, Alan?"

"No," I said, just to side with Andy, but I didn't sit down next to him to watch it, either.

"Poor Elvis," Cookie said, smiling. "That girl is already considering her options."

"You're imagining things," Andy said.

"Ask the boy."

"He's the King, right, Alan? Charley loves him." Andy gave me that sad puppy look, the one Lassie used to give me sometimes when I had to go off to school.

"I have a name," I said to Cookie, just in case he'd forgotten.

The old goat smiled at me. He looked smug. He liked the idea that I saw how rotten things were, just like he did. I didn't want to see things that way, but what could I do? Someone like Andy just fooled himself. Like my mom with her romances. Like my mom and how she kept trying to keep the peace in our family and see the best in everyone.

The problem with this was she pretended nothing was wrong when a whole lot was wrong.

Sometimes I thought maybe it was because her father had committed suicide. He'd been an alcoholic. He'd disappointed her a lot when she was a kid. Not shown up for birthdays and other occasions. Shown up drunk at her school once. That kind of stuff.

Then he killed himself when she was twenty.

Once I asked her about that, and she said he'd been drinking and had a bad day. I always thought that was a lame explanation. If I killed myself every time I had a bad day, I'd be dead about a thousand times.

**"G**o on," Cookie said. "Tell him."

"You think Cook's right, Alan?" Andy sounded worried.

What could I do? I wasn't my mother. I wasn't going to just pretend that I didn't see what was happening. "Yeah, she's going to leave him."

"You're wrong there, Alan," Andy said. He looked from me to Cookie. "You're both wrong."

I flopped down on the bed Andy wasn't on and closed my eyes. Cookie started in on Andy, saying he was a kind man but very foolish.

As I lay there I remembered this time when George had said something similar to my mother. We were visiting him in Chicago, eating at this fancy restaurant. One of his blond-haired girlfriends with lots of jewelry and a perfect face was along.

"You're a kind woman, Mom, but you're very foolish about the world. The real world isn't kind."

"All I was saying is not all those people living on the street are there because they're lazy. Some people have bad luck."

"Back me up, Dad. You know I'm right. You have to make your luck."

"You have to work hard," my father said, looking a little embarrassed. "I'm proud of how hard you've worked and the things you've accomplished."

My mother looked at the blonde, who kept staring at George like she thought he was a Greek hero.

"George was almost a straight A student all through school," my mother said proudly. "Even in college. The few Bs he got nearly killed him."

George smiled at her. You had to give George one thing. He never seemed embarrassed when my mother said something that should have sent the blood rushing to his face.

"You don't get to play with the big boys unless you can keep up. I'm right about that, aren't I, Susan?"

The blonde nodded like one of those little dogs in the back windows of cars. Anything George said was right to her.

"Nothing wrong with ambition," my father said, though, to be honest, he didn't sound as enthusiastic as he could have.

George looked at me and then at the blonde. "My little brother hasn't figured out what a tough world it is yet. He will. You can't start too far behind, Simon, or you'll never catch up."

"Maybe I don't want to catch up."

"That attitude worries me," George said, shaking his head.

I was about to tell him to worry about himself, but my mom put her hand on mine and I kept quiet.

George seemed encouraged by this, though. He started carrying on like he was a king. He ordered what he called the perfect wine. He ordered food for his girlfriend. He even ordered my parents' food. He would have ordered mine, but I wouldn't let him. I chose something off the menu I couldn't even pronounce. I didn't care.

George had an opinion on just about everything. Sports. Politics. Business, of course. I had to admit his arrogance could seem like confidence. I had to admit he was a success.

I was plenty ready when the time came to go back to the hotel room. We said our good-byes. Funny thing, George slipped me a hundred dollar bill when Mom and Dad weren't looking.

"Buy yourself something nice," he said.

What I couldn't figure out was why he slipped it to me. It was the kind of thing he liked to do in public to show how superior he was.

I guess I was a little thrown off by that. I didn't think I even said thanks. It sort of bothered me. Why it should bother me after all this time, I didn't know. What could it matter?

I slipped off into sleep. I guess because I was thinking about that night, I dreamed about it. I dreamed about my dad and mom talking to me on the elevator in the hotel. In the dream the elevator was glass, and we were going up and up and up way over the city. My dad said, "You don't have to be like your brother, Simon. You don't have to be like me. But you do have to be somebody. George is right. You can't just float along without any plan. You'll never get anywhere."

We kept getting higher and higher over the city. We were so high we might have been in a plane.

"Where's our room?" I asked my dad, scared to look down.

"George only gets the best for us. He's a good boy. We've got a room on the top of the world. What do you think about that?"

"He's a good boy," my mom said, nodding.

I got what they were saying. I'd heard it before from my father in many, many different ways. George was the good boy. Still, there was one thing that sort of weakened the effect of this: my father saying I didn't have to be like him or George. He'd never said anything like that to me before. It had always seemed to me he'd been saying, in one way or another, "My way or the highway."

I must have half woken up because I thought, *Well, I guess it turned out to be the highway.* But I was confused. What if he hadn't been saying that all along? What if I'd got it wrong?

## Love Me **Tender**

"Wake up, Alan," Elvis said, shaking me. "It's time."

My first thought, when I opened my eyes, was that I couldn't quite figure out if my father had really given me that little speech on the hotel elevator or if it only happened in the dream. It bothered me a little that I wasn't sure.

Everybody was in our room. Andy wore his best clothes. Charley kissed Andy on his quivering lips, and his face turned bright red.

"You go get her, Tiger. I'm going to stay here and watch a little TV and be alone for a few minutes. I'll be rooting for you."

Elvis tried to coax Charley into coming, but she said she needed to think things through. Andy tried to put off going by saying we could wait for another day when Charley could come along.

"You had better go ahead and get this over with, Andy," Cookie said, surprising us all.

Elvis drove south of the river down to the neighborhood Andy had left over twenty years ago. It took some driving around to find it. Once we did, it took a while to find the corner with the house on it. I kind of liked the house. It was old with tall windows and a tin roof.

"I think that's it," Andy said.

"You think?"

"It's been a long time."

The guy was just about wringing his hands. He was moments away from it.

A woman stepped out onto the porch carrying a rug. She shook the rug over the railing. Andy's face went white. It was just an old lady shaking a rug, but you would have thought he saw an alien or a ghost. She went back inside.

"I planted that pecan tree," he said, pointing to a big old tree in the side yard. "It was just a little pole."

He looked like he was about to cry.

"You can do this," I said.

Cookie put his hand on Andy's shoulder. "You better go on, Andy. You can find me down with those bums on that street we came in on."

"Guadalupe."

"That's the street. I'll be there. I'll wait around until I hear from you."

I thought Andy was going to kiss him, which wasn't something either Cookie or I wanted to see.

"Go on, now," Elvis said. "You go on, Andy."

"I wish I had me a drink. I love you boys. All of you. I want you to know that. And I hope we see one another real soon. I surely do."

Andy gave me a little hug; I tolerated it.

"Sing 'Love Me Tender,' will you, Elvis?" he said as he got out of the car.

Cookie shook his head. I shrugged like what did you expect from someone like Andy? All of a sudden Elvis began to sing. At first he sang kind of low, but then he let it out.

It was the voice of Elvis Aron Presley.

I should know, I'd had to listen to it enough times. I enjoyed smiling at Cookie, who frowned as if he had just found a spot on his suit.

Andy walked up the sidewalk and onto the porch. He knocked on the door.

"Susan?" he said. "It's me, Susan."

After a few seconds, the door opened slowly, and Andy stepped in.

Cookie had us take him up to Guadalupe. He wasn't nearly as sentimental about leaving as Andy had been.

"See you around" was all he said, and he stepped out of the car.

No "I love you guys" from Cookie. On the way back to the motel, Elvis got pretty worked up about how Cookie hadn't even said thank you. When we pulled into the parking lot, I told Elvis I was going to take a drive.

"You gonna go see him?"

"I'm going to try," I said.

"Maybe you want a little company? I don't mind goin' along with you."

I could see he was anxious to get back to Charley, though. I didn't blame him.

"You go on," I said. "I'll be back by tonight."

"We'll be here," he promised.

I wondered about that, though. I had the feeling that Charley was ready to move. I had the feeling Elvis was going to do what Charley wanted.

# It **Wasn't** in
## *The Illustrated History of Iowa*

I bought a map and found my way to the address in the phone book. The house was in a small field of knee-deep weeds at the end of a dead-end street. An old sports car, older than me I thought, was parked in the driveway. I parked in the street but left the engine running. What got me to shut it off finally was thinking about Andy. If a broken-down old guy like Andy could walk up to a house, I guess I could.

But when I got to the door, my arm rebelled and wouldn't raise my hand to ring the bell. I just stood there. I decided to walk around the house, circle it. A scouting mission.

My main thought was if I went to the door, this guy, my birth father or whatever, might say he didn't want any visit from any kid he'd left behind and slam the door in my face. If the guy did that, I would pretty much have to leave.

And that would be it. After all I'd gone through to get to meet him, it would be over with. Then what would I do?

I looked in the first window I came to. The living room. It had a set of furniture that looked like it might have been in the showroom of a furniture store not too long ago. The place was pretty junky: beer bottles, overturned ashtrays, and scattered newspapers.

If my mom saw that room, she would go half crazy. She would know immediately that the people who lived there were lost souls. My mom pretty much decided that one thing heaven had to be was neat and clean.

I should have gone back to the front door after I window-peeped, but I continued moving around the house. I opened the gate to the backyard. When I tried to shut it, the metal latch bumped against the catch, and the door swung against the house. I froze but didn't hear anyone shout or anything, so I peeked in the bedroom window. It was kind of dark in there, but I saw a woman pulling on a pair of tight jeans, working her butt into them. She didn't have a shirt on, and I sort of lingered. "She's got great tits, don't she?" a voice behind me said.

It was a friendly voice, but when I swung around, I saw a tall man holding a baseball bat. At first I had this crazy idea he wanted to play baseball with me. That was something a dad did with his son, right? Go out into the street and play a little ball. "I wasn't looking," I said. Not one of the smartest things I've ever said.

"What exactly are you doing, kid?"

That would take a lot of explaining.

"I'm from Iowa," I said, when what I really wanted to say was *Don't you recognize me?*

He squinted like he was looking into the sun and said, "Okay, Iowa, let's go inside and talk for a minute."

I waited for him to lead the way, but he motioned with the bat for me to go first. I kind of paused a moment.

"Go on, Iowa. We wouldn't want one of my nosy neighbors to call the police now, would we?"

It seemed to me that he wouldn't mind them calling the police if he really thought I was a peeper. It was just a small thing, but it was my first hint that my dad—or whatever you wanted to call him—wasn't at ease with authority. I led the way inside.

The woman I had seen in the bedroom was sitting on the living room sofa smoking a cigarette. She wore a tight, black T-shirt with a picture of a Harley-Davidson on the front. Dean told me to have a seat. I sat down next to the woman, who smiled a big, toothy smile.

"This is Iowa, honey. Iowa, Claire," Dean said.

"My name is Alan." I didn't need any more aliases.

I couldn't help noticing that Claire's breasts looked pretty good in a T-shirt, too. "Tell me about Iowa," Dean said, like maybe he thought it was a code word for something.

There are eight pigs for every person. The thought just popped into my head. Fortunately, it didn't spill out of my mouth for a change. "You lived there once," I said.

This wasn't a fact from *The Illustrated History of Iowa* or a book like that, and he looked me over like he thought he might have missed something.

"Maybe," he said.

"You had a kid there."

I looked at the woman. She was a lot younger than Dean, but her eyes were nervous and watchful and hard.

"What did you say your name was?" Dean asked. He was still standing and still holding the bat.

"Alan."

We stared at each other. I guess he was looking for the same thing I was looking for. I saw it. Dark hair, high cheekbones, big nose. His eyebrows were thick like mine. He had long, straight hair held back in a ponytail. That was different. I could never grow a good ponytail because my hair was too curly.

"I drove a long way," I said. I didn't mention the circumstances. I didn't tell him, "You're my last hope," or anything. But that was what I felt.

At first he kept silent. Then he laughed. You had to like his laugh because it made you want to laugh, too. I never laughed like that. I would have liked to, but I didn't.

"I'll be damned. After all this time, you came looking for me." He shook his head like that was about the craziest thing he'd heard in a long time. Still, he was smiling. He seemed to like crazy things.

Dean dropped the bat on a chair and walked over to the dining room table. He picked up a half-empty bottle of Jack Daniel's, screwed off the cap, and took a drink. Then he handed the bottle to me.

"You mean this is your kid?" Claire said, sitting up straight for the first time. "You told me you didn't have no kids."

Not accusing exactly, but close.

"I never expected the baby I left in Iowa to grow up and come looking for me. It's a surprise, Claire. Look at him. Can't be even eighteen, and here he is. You got to admit this wasn't something I could foresee."

I took a drink from the Jack Daniel's and handed it back to Dean. Claire looked from Dean to me. It was a little strange to be drinking Jack Daniel's with a guy Dean's age who also happened to be my—what was he? Dad didn't seem right. Anyway, I already had a dad. I felt a stab of guilt thinking about that.

"I got to get to work," Claire said, putting out her cigarette in an overflowing ashtray. She didn't look too pleased by our reunion.

"You go on then, honey," Dean said, but he was looking at me when he said it. "Alan and I will get acquainted."

"You coming by the club later?"

"Sure."

"You gonna bring the kid?"

"Maybe."

"Keep him at one of the back tables. Mike had the cops in the other night, and he ain't in a good mood."

She got up and strutted over to Dean and took his face in her hands and forced a hard kiss on his lips, like she was taking back possession of him or maybe just reminding him she had a few things no new kid, son or no son, had.

She messed up my hair with her hand on the way out. I didn't think she liked me, but then she did that, and it confused me. When she left, I asked Dean what kind of club she worked in, and he said a strip joint.

We sat down and he took a drink and handed the bottle to me, and I took a drink. We didn't say anything. I tried not to stare, but I couldn't help it. See, here was this guy who was my dad—but wasn't. I felt something just looking at him, and at the same time he was a stranger. But my dad at home was kind of a stranger, too. I mean, I knew him well enough. He had always been in my life, but we didn't like to do the same things. We weren't alike. If we weren't related, we wouldn't have a thing in common.

"Let's go for a drive, Alan," Dean said, jumping up. "I want to show you something."

I shrugged and followed along, which he seemed to think kind of funny.

"Just like a teenager," he said.

I didn't know who he thought he was talking to. Not me. He carried the bottle out to his beat-up sports car. I had to help him pull back the convertible roof. Duct tape held together a big tear in the plastic of the rear window.

He drove fast. We raced through city streets. Yellow lights and lights turning red meant hit the gas to Dean. The wind rushed over us. We entered an interstate and then got off it again. We passed through a lot of sprawling city. He pointed out landmarks. Most of them were bars. A few were places where he had made a good bet or met someone named Heather, Sara, Sue Ann, Desiree, and a few others.

Then we were out of the city completely. It was not what I thought of when I thought of Texas. No tumbleweeds or desert hills and cacti. No cowboys moseying along behind dusty cows. The rolling hills were spotted with houses, and the highway followed a slow-moving emerald river. Finally, we came to a lake tucked away in those hills. We drove along a narrow gravel road that cut back about ten times before ending at a parking lot close to the lake. Then we had to climb down some rocks to get to the large, round, flat rocks down by the water where people sat and lay, some of them without clothes. The sun made wrinkles of light in the lake.

We sat on a big rock, and Dean took a drink of whiskey and handed me the bottle. I didn't feel much like more whiskey, but I drank. It burned going down my throat. Sometimes I didn't have a clue why I did a thing. I just did it.

"How'd you find me, kid?"

"There was a paper with my birth certificate that had your name on it and where you were from. It said Austin, Texas."

"That's something," he said. "You drove all this way with just that?"

"It was kind of on my way to California." Anyone with even the vaguest sense of geography wasn't going to be taken in by that one. He let it go, though.

"I expect you got girlfriends," he said, which sort of surprised me. I mean, there were a lot of things we could have talked about. Girlfriends surprised me.

"I had one, but she died in a car accident. She was all disfigured and stuff first. It was pretty tragic."

"Sorry to hear that," he said, but he didn't sound all that sorry. It made me a little mad. I could have had a girlfriend who died in a car wreck. If I had had one like that, I would expect a little more sympathy than "Sorry to hear that."

Maybe I was a little mad, anyway. Not a reason in the world why I should have been. Dean liked to drink, and I liked to drink. He didn't seem to care much for laws, and neither did

I. If I told Dean I had trouble with authority, he'd probably slap me on the back and say he knew exactly what I meant.

"I have always loved women," Dean said. "My first little girlfriend was this thirteen-year-old. Her hair was so blond it was almost white, and she had that drawl they have in the Deep South. Man, that was something. I was thirteen myself. I thought I was in heaven."

I imagined he was going to tell me about a lot of women. I wasn't any Don Juan, though, and I wasn't all that impressed by Don Juan stories.

"Iowa," he said, "was a place I never expected to stay for more than a day. I won a lot of money in a poker game in Chicago. I drove west thinking I would go to California, but I stopped in Iowa City for the night. It was amazing how many girls that little college town had. I couldn't leave.

"I got in with this group that had a farm down by Mansfield. The guy that owned the farm had three wives. His name was Big Dawg. That's what he called himself. Big Dawg had connections down South, and he hired me to pick up loads of dope in this little village in central Mexico. That was my life over the next two years. I'd go pick up marijuana down in Mexico, stop off in Texas to visit friends, and drive back to Iowa, where Big Dawg would distribute the marijuana all over the Midwest. It was a sweet operation. That was a good time. I made a lot of money."

This was Dean's idea of success. I'd been in the same line of work before I left Iowa, so I couldn't say there was anything wrong with it. I mean, it could be a little depressing at times, but the money was good. To be honest, I think the main reason I sold marijuana wasn't money. It was because it made people notice me.

Or maybe it was in my genes. You heard experts arguing that nature-versus-nurture question all the time, but they didn't really know.

It was like the weather people when they didn't have any idea what the weather was up to. They'd look right into the camera without a hint of shame and say, "There is about a 50 percent chance of rain today." Like we were supposed to be impressed by their forecasting prowess. Most of these so-called experts, these psychologist types, ended up saying a person was about 50 percent nature and about 50 percent nurture. Right.

"And that was when you met my mother," I said.

It just came out. See, I knew exactly how my dad in Iowa had met my mom. How they had met in high school, dated, and married that summer after they graduated. And how they had been together so long they kind of even looked like each other. And how even when my friends' parents were getting divorced, I never worried too much about mine. I couldn't imagine one without the other. I was outside of what they had, though. I could imagine me without them. I guess that was how I could leave.

"No," he said. "Kate and I met here in Texas. Guess your roots are here in Texas, too. Kate grew up in Dallas, and I grew up out in West Texas."

That was something I hadn't thought about. I could have grown up drinking quarts of tea and calling my father Daddy.

What would it have been like? It was someone else's life.

"We got reacquainted on one of my trips down to Mexico for Big Dawg. I stopped in Austin, and she and I fell in serious love again. She went back to Iowa with me. We really tried to make it work. Rented ourselves a little farm and everything."

"Tried to make it work?" I said. My mind was moving like I'd sprained something in there.

"We loved each other," he said.

"Where is she?"

"Don't know. We stayed together until you were born, and then we went to California and split up. It was just like that Dylan song. We split up on the docks one night both agreeing it was best. Like that. I heard later she hooked up with a millionaire. A Frenchman, I think it was. I heard she moved to France."

"What was she like?" I whispered. I could hardly hear myself. My throat became dry as dust the moment I asked the question.

"She was a beautiful woman. She liked to have a good time. We had some good times, but she could give a man hell. She could be tough. You looked into those eyes and you saw fire sometimes. She loved life. Truth is, neither of us was much good at the long-distance run. We were sprinters. Love ain't always enough for sprinters, Alan."

He emphasized the word *ain't* to let me know he knew better than to use it but went ahead anyway. He smiled like he was making a joke, but his smile got kind of sad. He took a drink of whiskey.

"You look like her, but I can see some of me, too," he said.

I tried to look into Dean's eyes, but they were so full of him, there wasn't room for me. I don't know. I wished I hadn't thought this. I wanted to see myself in Dean. I wanted to imagine the woman he was talking about and see myself in her, because I'd never seen myself in anyone.

It made me lonely sometimes. Other people looked like someone. Their father, uncle, aunt, cousin. My dad and mom both had family they looked like. When my parents' families got together, I felt more lonely than ever. It was like I didn't come from anywhere, and I didn't belong anywhere.

"Maybe she's not in France," I said.

"Hard to say. Yep. You got me in you. Blood tells. My old man used to say that. He used to say I would straighten out someday because blood tells."

"You get along with your father?"

"Not really," he said. "I'd have to say no."

I'd have to say no, too. My dad could fix about anything, but he had given up on fixing me. It was funny, but as soon as I thought this, I remembered a time before he'd given up. I was twelve or thirteen, and I helped him build a deck on a house he was finishing in North Liberty. It took us the whole weekend.

Afterward we sat on the steps of the deck and drank Hy-Vee ginger ales, which he liked and I thought tasted like weeds and sugar water. He slapped me on the back and smiled at me the same way he used to smile at my older brother, George, when George handed him a report card with all As.

"Look what you did. You helped me build the whole thing. Feels good, doesn't it? That sense of accomplishment."

"Sure," I said.

I could see he was disappointed by my lack of enthusiasm. Then he said, "Wasn't that fun?"

Even then, when I didn't have a thought of leaving, I couldn't get excited about building things. "Yeah, it was okay."

My dad told me he'd always wanted to be a contractor and hoped someday I might want the same. We could go into business together.

I'd looked away, my face feeling hot, and drank that sugar water and weeds like I loved it. When I looked back at him, he was already up and loading tools into his toolbox.

It was funny, but a part of me wished I could go back to that day and pretend that building decks was just about the most thrilling thing in the world. I knew it wouldn't change anything. I just wanted to see my dad smile at me that way one last time.

It was strange to be sitting across from Dean thinking about my dad. The thing was, only a year or two after we built that deck together, things started going bad between us. We weren't on the same side anymore. Shouldn't we have been on the same side? I guess you could just about fill up the world with the things that should have been.

He was always telling me what I was doing wrong. He would complain about the way I looked, dressed, spoke, the music I listened to, the books I read, about my friends, my interests and lack of interests. I blew up pretty often. We had some shouting matches.

After a while we didn't talk much. He was always letting me know how I'd let him down, though. All I had to do was look at him across the dinner table to see how he felt.

"I don't get along with mine, either," I said.

Dean looked at me kind of funny. Maybe because he'd forgotten I'd been raised by someone. Like maybe he thought I'd been in some incubator all this time and just popped out full grown and come looking for him.

About this time I noticed a muscular guy paddling a big inflatable raft toward us. A woman with melon breasts sat on the raft. (I don't want anyone thinking I had a thing about breasts, but if they were there, they weren't something you could ignore.) The guy was paddling pretty hard with his hands, water splashing every time he slapped the water. He looked red in the face.

"Dean," I said, "do you know that guy?"

Dean looked over at the guy.

"Dean," the man shouted.

"Time to go, Alan. Places to go, people to see."

He got up real fast, and I did, too.

"Dean," the man shouted again.

Dean waved. "Nice to see you."

He ran up the trail, and I ran after him. He was fast for an old guy.

"Goddamnit, Dean," the man shouted.

At the top of the rocks, I looked back to see where the man was. He was no longer on the raft. Now he was running up the trail, buck-naked.

Dean had the car started by the time I got to it. I jumped

in. I kind of liked that. I felt a little James Bondish. I almost fell out when Dean put the car in reverse. The tires screeched. The angry, naked man came running across the parking lot.

"Who was that?" I asked when we were back on the road and Angry, Naked Guy was nowhere to be seen.

"Haven't a clue," he said.

We sped back the same way we had come. Dean seemed to speed everywhere. Even when he sat still, he tapped his feet and moved his hands a lot.

Anyway, I hoped we didn't run into any more naked, screaming guys Dean didn't know.

# He **Enjoyed** Being Crazy

We drove to a little bar in a neighborhood I wasn't too crazy to be in. There were people sitting out on the stoops of dilapidated houses, the kind with sagging porches, broken windows, and missing pieces of siding. These people looked like they spent most of their time right where they were. We pulled up into the drive of a small building made of cinder blocks. No windows.

"I have to place a little bet on the game," Dean said.

"In there?"

"Yeah, come on."

I got out of the car and followed him into the bar. It was one of those hole-in-the-wall type of bars. A big fat guy sat at a table in the corner. You could see the rolls of his belly through his knit sport shirt. He was Hispanic. Another Hispanic guy stood behind the bar. He made the first big guy look like a dwarf. He also had the longest mustache I'd ever seen.

"Dean, my man," the guy at the table said.

"Good to see you, Marcos. You look good. Like you lost some weight maybe. Been hitting the gym?"

"I'm on this damn diet," he said. "I been running around Town Lake. Hate it. Sally goes with me. He hates it, too."

The guy behind the bar nodded. Sally was a strange name for a guy, but looking at him, I didn't feel the need to point this out. I doubted many people did.

"This is my son," Dean said. Then to me, "These are my good friends, Alan."

The guy sitting at the table said, "I didn't know you had a kid, Dean."

"Here he is."

The big guy standing behind the bar reminded me of this movie I'd seen about Pancho Villa.

"You must have brought your son to show him how a man settles his debts. Am I right?"

"Sure, Marcos, you know I'm going to pay. Soon as I close this deal. I'm inches away. I'm telling you, inches."

"What's he been telling us for the past few weeks, Sally?"

"Inches. Inches away."

Sally's voice was high, almost like a girl's.

"And I was telling you the truth. Tonight's the night. I'm getting the check at this party, and tomorrow I'll bring you the cash."

"Tomorrow?" Marcos said. "I'm glad to hear you say that. Tomorrow. We're glad, aren't we, Sally?"

Sally didn't say anything. If I had a voice like that, I guess I wouldn't talk all that much, either.

"He likes you, Dean. He would have hated to break your arms and legs, but business is business. I'm sure you've heard that before."

"Absolutely. No problem whatsoever. You have to make a living, but since we're all clear about what's going to happen tomorrow, how about putting five big ones on the basketball game tonight?"

Marcos laughed. His belly shook when he laughed. Sort of like a mobster Santa Claus.

"Guy owes me thirty and wants me to put another five on a game. You got balls, Dean. I'll give you that."

"Okay, maybe five's too much," Dean said. "Two."

Marcos shook his head. "I'll see you tomorrow. Then we'll talk about your next bet."

Dean looked like he was sorry for Marcos or something, like he felt bad Marcos wasn't looking out for his business better.

"Okay, your loss, Marcos."

Marcos stopped smiling. "Tomorrow, Dean. No more games."

"Absolutely, tomorrow. Without a doubt. You can depend on it."

Dean turned around and walked out the door. I had to hurry to keep up with him. I expected him to be all upset when I got outside, but he was laughing. We got in the car, and he was still laughing.

"I almost had the son of a bitch," he said. "Can you believe it? Guy like Marcos almost went for it."

That wasn't the way I saw it, but I had to admit I felt like laughing. Dean all happy because he'd almost conned a guy who probably didn't get conned much. I don't know. Maybe it was his laugh. He got his shoulders into it, and it was musical. I had to laugh with him.

He was crazy, I guess, but he liked being crazy. Maybe I was crazy, too, but I couldn't get his enjoyment out of it.

He backed out of the drive and squealed the tires as he took off down the street.

# She's **Defying** Gravity

Dean knew a place, not surprisingly, where the happy hour started earlier than usual. It was called the Kit Kat Lounge. We stopped by for refreshments, as Dean called them. I started calling them that, too. Dean knew the bartender at the Kit Kat, and some of the people sitting at the bar. He greeted them with his usual enthusiasm. I tried to be enthusiastic when I spoke to whoever he introduced me to.

Dean ordered a Tecate with lime, and I ordered the same. We talked to this woman at the bar who sang in a band that Dean said was very popular in Austin. Dean didn't even know her, but within minutes she'd offered to put his name and mine on some list that would get us in free to the Continental Club, where she was playing on Friday. Dean seemed to have a way of making people want to do things for him, especially women.

After she left, Dean and I played pool. He held his cue differently than I did. He liked to put his index finger and little finger on the cushion and raise his thumb and let the cue rest over the thumb. I tried it. I missed about four shots before I made a ball, but Dean didn't do much better. It was a long game. Dean was a bad pool player. I wasn't usually a bad pool player, but I was that afternoon because I was trying to shoot like Dean.

Dean let me drive to our next stop, and I peeled out and ran every light that was yellow or recently red. He directed me to a place called Honey's, the club where Claire worked.

The music attacked you when you walked in. It was a pounding disco beat. The entryway was so dark, it was hard to see what was in front of you. It got a little lighter around the corner but not much. A laser shot around the room, and there were some dull lights behind the bar.

A guy at a podium looked like a linebacker stuffed into a suit. He nodded at Dean. Dean nodded back.

"Go on in," he said. He stopped these guys behind us and told them the cover charge was three bucks.

A girl was dancing on a large round stage with a brass bar in the middle that went from the floor to the ceiling. She wore a G-string and high, pointy heels. There were other girls walking around or sitting at tables with guys.

I tried to look as cool as Dean, but I was a little uncomfortable. I don't know. I worked on smiling the way he smiled, but the problem was, I had to fake it. He didn't. Nothing seemed to disturb or upset him. I doubted I could ever be like that.

A lot of the girls knew Dean and made a fuss over him, and they made a fuss over me, too, since I was with him.

We found a table near the back and ordered beers. Some girls sat at our table while Claire danced. Even though she had these beautiful breasts, I was embarrassed. I couldn't help it. She kept posing, trying to look all sexy. She sort of did at first, but then she kept doing the same poses over and over again. What was most embarrassing, though, was that she was a terrible dancer. She seemed to hardly notice the music.

Dean just talked and talked, and the girls at the table loved it. You could tell. He was handsome. I mean, for an old guy. But it wasn't just that. He was real comfortable around them, and he made them laugh.

After a while, the girls wandered off to paying customers. Some of them seemed genuinely sorry to go.

We drank two more Tecates with lime and Dean told me about whorehouses in Mexico and Europe and he crabbed about how prostitution should be legal in the States. Society shouldn't make girls criminals just because they were trying to earn a living. He seemed to feel strongly about this issue. I said he was right. He was, I guess, but it wasn't an issue right up there with civil rights or anything. You would have thought so listening to Dean.

Dean bought a pack of cigarettes and lit one up. "I like to smoke from time to time, but I don't let myself get too attached to it. That's the trick with addiction. You have to keep it under control."

That didn't sound right to me. If you were addicted to something, didn't that mean you'd lost control? But Dean said everything with such confidence, you just kind of accepted it.

"A cigarette every now and then is good for you," Dean said, handing me one.

I knew this probably wasn't true, either, but on the other hand, scientists were always changing their minds about what was good and bad for people. I took the cigarette.

We blew smoke rings for a while, until I had a coughing fit. I put my cigarette out then. Dean finished his.

A new dancer came onstage. Dean seemed enthused by her enormous breasts, breasts larger even than the woman's on the raft with the naked man Dean didn't know.

"What do you think about those?" he said, shaking his head, his face lighting up like he was witnessing some wonder of nature.

I smiled and shook my head, too, but then he said it again, "Huh? What about those?"

At first I'd thought it was just one of those rhetorical questions guys ask guys about certain anatomical features of girls. But when he asked the second time, I thought he was really asking me. I was a little drunk.

"I don't understand how she can stay standing up, to tell you the truth. Seems like she'd have to keep picking herself up off the floor."

"But aren't they a work of art?"

"It's like she's defying gravity."

He seemed puzzled by my reaction. He looked at me kind of funny, like he was trying to figure out if I was clever or ridiculous. I think he decided on ridiculous.

But even if he didn't, I think he was pretty sure about one thing: I wasn't cool. Somehow I hadn't got the cool gene from him. I thought about this while the girl with the breasts that were a work of art tried to climb the pole on the stage.

You'd think I'd be upset about not being cool, but I wasn't. The truth was, admitting this to myself was a relief.

Claire sat down with us. She and Dean kissed. She looked over her shoulder as soon as they were finished, like she was worried about something.

"I can't stay long," she said. "Mike's in a mood. You know how he gets."

She turned to me and asked what I thought of the club. I said it was pretty interesting. She laughed.

"It's his first time," Dean said. "He'll get used to it. Then I won't be able to get him out of here."

Maybe I could get used to it. I guess you could get used to just about anything.

Only the thing was, and it was kind of a surprise to me, I wasn't sure I wanted to.

# Like the **Sundance Kid**

We left Honey's the way Dean left everyplace. He decided it was time and jumped up, and off we went. He drove us back to his house because he had to make an important phone call.

"This is a life-or-death phone call," he told me as we walked in. "You pray for me now, Alan."

Then he told me to watch some TV, so I guess he wasn't serious about the praying, which was a good thing because I wouldn't have known where to start.

After about fifteen minutes, Dean came out of the bedroom all happy. He was wearing a suit, and he said we were going to the mall. Just like that, he was out the door. I was getting pretty tired of running after him, but that was the way he was. You weren't going to gain any weight hanging around Dean.

"Aren't you a little old to hang out at the mall?" I asked him.

"I like wit," he said. "You're a witty kid. God, was I ever as young as you?"

There he went again asking a question I was sure was rhetorical, but he waited for an answer. I didn't give him one. I wondered if I would tell him to go to hell if I had someplace else to go, say for example I was on my way to California or Florida or Africa.

"I don't like mall food," I said. I noticed it was past dinnertime. Past the time my parents ate dinner, anyway. Six o'clock and food was on the table in their house. You could have timed a rocket launch by it.

"We're going to get you a suit," he said.

I told him I wasn't the suit type, but he ignored me. When we got to the store in the mall, I told the clerk the same thing, since Dean seemed unable to comprehend what I was saying.

"Isn't that just the way these kids are today," Dean said to the salesman, who gave us one of those lip smiles. I hate a lip smile. And I didn't care much for being called a kid, either.

"We need a suit he can walk out of the store in," Dean said.

"Why?" I said. "Why do I need a suit?"

"Going to a party." Dean looked through a rack of gray suits. The hangers made an irritating sound as they moved across the metal rod.

"I'm not much for parties."

"Beth wants to meet you. I told her about you when I called from the house, and now she wants to meet you. Get to know you a little. This could work out very well for us."

"My mother? Beth, my mother?" He hadn't said anything about a Beth before, so I got momentarily confused. It was stupid.

"Your mother's name is Kate," he reminded me. "I'm talking about my fiancée, Beth."

I didn't ask him about Claire. I hadn't known Dean for long, but I'd known him long enough I didn't need to ask.

Dean made me go try the suit on. When I came out of the dressing room, Dean was talking to a saleswoman across the aisle in lingerie. She was laughing.

"What a handsome young man," she said.

"You clean up real good, Alan," Dean said.

The saleswoman looked like she was probably in college. I noticed he didn't tell her I was his son, and I noticed he got her phone number before we left. On the ride back to the house he told me there would be a lot of very rich people at this party and this Beth woman was going to write him a check for a business they were starting. My role, he said, was to help him reassure her that her money was in safe hands.

"She's a little nervous," he said. "She wants us to get married before we start our little business. Your coming gave me an idea. I told her I couldn't because of you. It was my little confession to her that I had a son. I was good, Alan. I was Robert fucking De Niro. She forgave me right away."

"What do you mean because of me?" I didn't get it. Maybe because I didn't want to.

"I told her how I raised you on my own. See, you're already good luck for me. She's going to do it now. She thinks I'm more responsible than I seem. I must be if I raised a kid. A hundred grand, Alan. Seed money for our real-estate investment group."

"This is your fiancée we're talking about?" I said.

He looked like he wasn't sure I was serious.

"This is what I do," he said as he ran another red light.

"What do you do?"

"I thought you understood. I'm a confidence man, Alan. A gambler and a confidence man. Sometimes I win at gambling and sometimes I lose, but I have always been able to find women to give me money."

"And I'm what? Your partner or something?" I said. A part of me was—I don't know—flattered.

"You're my son." He slammed on the brakes to avoid rear-ending a truck that had stopped at a light recently turned red.

Dean fumed. "Damn little town driver. That's the kind of guy who causes accidents. Never ever be that kind of driver, Alan."

I took a deep breath. "What do I have to do?"

I wanted to please him. I couldn't help myself. It was like I got sometimes with my dad up in Iowa. I'd help him fix something like, say, the gutter on the house or a leaky faucet, and he'd get all excited about it and tell me I was a lot of help. And I'd sort of be proud in spite of myself. Then he'd ruin it by saying something like "You can do it if you want to." First off, we weren't talking about climbing Mt. Everest or brain surgery. And second, the truth was, I didn't much want to do that stuff. He liked to do it, but it didn't make me lazy or crazy that I didn't.

"You have to lie well. Try to think about the way it might have been if I had raised you. Well, not me exactly, the successful businessman recently fallen on hard times that Beth thinks I am. You can do this, Alan. You're imaginative. You just have to use that imagination. Work the truth in with a lie. Makes it more convincing. Then we'll be off to my favorite place in Mexico for a few weeks. You and me. We'll have fun."

I compared Dean's ambitions for me with my father's. My father's: work hard, fix things, build things, save money, keep my room clean, get good grades. Dean's: lie well, con people out of money, go to Mexico, drink a lot, have many girlfriends.

"Your father didn't have much imagination, did he?" I said, thinking about my father.

"My daddy didn't have a lick of imagination to him. His way or the highway. He wore my mom out with his way. I'll tell you that much, Alan. My mom was a saint, but even a saint couldn't survive a man who was always right."

"You never got along with your father?" I said.

I wasn't about to call anyone Daddy. It wasn't easy for me to even listen to a man call his father Daddy. I sure wasn't going to ever take it up. I could live in Texas for twenty years, and I wasn't going to do that.

"That's the understatement of understatements, kid."

I was getting pretty tired of being called kid.

"You can call me Alan," I said.

"What?"

"My name. Not kid."

"It's affectionate. Like the Sundance Kid. Like that."

Except this wasn't a Western, we weren't living in any movie, and I wasn't some fast-draw type. I wasn't an outlaw. Well, not exactly. I was sort of a fugitive, but only in a minor way. No one was going to hang me or write books about Simon the Kid, who stole his father's car and drove to Texas.

"You want me to go to this party?" I said.

We had a short staring match, which made me a little nervous since he was driving.

"Christ," he said. "Okay. Okay, Alan. Fine. I'm going to give you a little spending money if you do a good job for me tonight. One thousand dollars."

"I want two," I said.

He smiled. "That's my boy."

# **Your Daddy** Is a Prince

On the drive out I admitted to Dean I didn't really like rich people. He didn't take this too well.

"Everyone always says that, but what they really mean is they don't like rich people because they aren't rich themselves."

"That's not what I mean," I said.

He looked skeptical. "You're way too young for all that sixties crap."

I guessed Dean wasn't going to help me take on the advertisers of the world or anything like that.

"Anyway," he said, not looking all that happy to have me sitting beside him, "you better pretend you like them tonight."

"I will," I promised too quickly.

I guess I thought Dean was like a second chance. Dean and I could be friends. We could drink Jack Daniel's and drive around in his sports car and go out to the lake and maybe swim and talk about stuff. Dean and I had a lot in common. And if we hadn't really talked about anything much below the surface yet, it was probably because we didn't really know each other or just hadn't had the time.

Sure, Dean moved fast and didn't like to linger, but that didn't mean he couldn't. We would have a lot to talk about later.

My dad and I had nothing to talk about.

Now, my dad's mother was a different story. We joked around a lot, and we laughed at the same things. She didn't mind a sarcastic remark or two. She could see how a lot of the world was messed up and didn't try to pretend otherwise.

Also, she liked some things I liked. She liked novels and professional wrestling, for instance. She liked to roller-skate, and we would go downtown and roller-skate sometimes. She had a kind of sparkle to her.

When we used to go visit, she would always make a fuss over me, and my dad would say, "Don't make too much of him. You'll give him the wrong ideas."

By wrong ideas he meant I shouldn't think I was special. I should understand I wasn't. At least that was what I thought he meant.

I really missed her when she died about four years ago, a couple of months before Lassie died. I really felt bad.

Her funeral was the first and only time I ever saw my dad cry.

"She liked you," he said afterward when we were driving home.

"I loved her."

"That's not what I mean. She loved you, too, but she also liked you, being around you, talking to you. She and I never got along that way. I wish we had."

"She loved you," my mom said to my dad, taking his hand.

"I know," he said. "I know that but not like with him. She had the craziest ideas on how to live. He's just like her. But she could light up a room, couldn't she? She had a light in her."

I guess I never thought of it before, but Grandma and my dad were like my dad and me in that we weren't much alike.

"She loved you," my mom said again. No one said anything else the rest of the way home.

The party was as bad as I thought it would be. It was in a house that Dean said had twelve bedrooms. It was probably four times the size of my parents' house. A guy at this big iron gate had to let us in because there was a wall all around the place.

What I noticed about Dean was that he had no trouble fitting right in with these people. He seemed as relaxed around them as he'd been around Marcos and Sally and the girls at that club and the salesgirl at the mall.

I wasn't relaxed at all. I would have preferred to be just about anyplace else. Some old guy wearing a tuxedo and cowboy boots and drinking whiskey pulled me off to the side and said, "Your daddy is one hell of a man, son. He and I had us a good time down in Mexico. He took me to a beautiful place."

This old guy had one of those red faces that made him look as if he had just recently been holding his breath. He lit a smelly cigar and blew smoke in my face.

"He took you to his favorite place?" I said.

"Oh yeah. Had us a good old time. I can drink, boy. I can drink most men under the table, but I had a hard time keeping up with your daddy."

He made this sound like the ultimate compliment. Like Dean was some kind of Olympic athlete or something and this guy, while world class, wasn't quite up to Dean's level.

The guy let his ashes fall on the rug. He touched a waiter's arm as he passed by. "Boy, get me another, will you? Glenlivet, no water."

He scratched his chin and smiled at one of the many short-skirted, beautiful women in the room. She smiled an obligatory smile back but quickly looked away. I half expected this guy to pull a lasso out of his jacket and rope her.

"Did you do something for him?" I knew this wasn't the most diplomatic question in the world.

"Oh, not really. Introduced him to a few people. You know, helped him get back on his feet again."

This old guy looked me over just to make sure he hadn't missed anything. He seemed to regret what he'd said, but he wasn't one to ponder mistakes too long.

"Your daddy is a prince," he said. "You just remember that. A prince."

His royal highness came up and told me Beth wanted to meet me. He winked at the old guy.

"Hey, young man," the old guy said as Dean and I walked away. "A prince."

"What was that all about?" Dean asked.

"He thinks you're royalty because you can drink more than he can."

Dean smiled his royal smile. "I'm a pretty good drinker. We get to Mexico, I'll show you how to tie one on. How to have a good time. You'll have two thousand dollars to spend. You can have a lot of fun in Mexico on two thousand."

"You said a trip to Mexico," I said, thinking about how he'd taken that old guy to his favorite place. He'd made it sound like I was special, but I could see that wasn't the way it was. "You didn't say anything about me spending my money."

I saw a glitter queen coming our way. She was wearing one of those dresses that sparkles. She had pretty blond hair held on the top of her head with pins. She was older. A little older than Dean, probably, but well preserved. She looked a little like Trinity's mother, which didn't exactly predispose me to liking her.

"Don't quibble," he said.

"You said you would take me to your favorite spot. The two thousand was something else."

Beth stopped to say something to a tall woman with big hair. The tall woman laughed a big horsy laugh.

"We'll talk about it later."

"I can't work under these conditions," I said, like I was a temperamental actor about to walk out on a production.

Dean glared at me, but Beth was only a few feet away from us by then. She gave me a big smile. He could see I was holding back.

"Okay," Dean said. "Okay, kid. You win."

I smiled and waved. She liked that. She liked me. I didn't have to do a thing, but I did anyway.

"I'm pleased to meet you, ma'am," I said.

We shook hands and made polite conversation. Small talk. Then she made her move. It was too fast for me to stop, and it was too fast for Dean to stop, too.

"I need a hand getting some things in the kitchen," she said, grabbing my arm. She had quite a grip. "I need a strong young man. We'll be right back, Dean."

"Can I help?" Dean said.

"You're too old." She smiled at me. "I need a younger man."

I looked over my shoulder at Dean, who didn't seem any happier than I was by the turn of events. In fact, he looked like he was about to run after us, but some guy shouted his name from across the room, and he was distracted just long enough that Beth could push me through one of those swinging doors restaurants have between dining rooms and kitchens. And that was where we were, in a kitchen about the size of my parents' living room. It was pretty active in there. Waiters rushing around with trays and food and drinks and a cook over by a sink arguing with a boy washing pots and pans.

Beth led me out the back of the kitchen and through several rooms. We stopped in front of the first closed door.

"I hope you don't mind," she said. "I wanted us to have a few minutes to talk alone."

"I don't mind at all," I said, which didn't have one strand of truth to it.

"This is my private room." She opened one of those fancy little black purses and pulled out a key.

The room was the smallest I'd seen in her house. It didn't have much in it: a reading chair and lamp, a small desk in the corner, and bookcases with books (without, I noticed, covers of handsome men and beautiful women gazing longingly at each other). The other thing it had was paintings on the wall. I liked these paintings. They were all of interesting places, though not all were pretty. All were set outdoors.

"This is my special room," she said. "Not even your father has seen this room."

It did have only one chair, so he wouldn't have had a place to sit, anyway.

"It's nice," I said, because she seemed to be waiting for something.

"I know your father and you have had a hard time," she said.

She didn't realize how confusing that statement was to me. She didn't know it was like she was talking to me about my Iowa father and not Dean, who was and wasn't my father.

You could look at it like I had two fathers now, but it felt like I didn't have any. One I had left behind, and one I hadn't gotten to. The truth was, Dean just didn't seem like a real father. That was crazy, I know. What was a real father? I caught myself thinking of my Iowa father. I could hear his voice all the way from Iowa telling me I knew right from wrong.

"I don't want to come between you and your father," she said. "I want to be a friend to you."

"Dean and I had a talk about you two getting married." I tried but failed at a smile. It just wouldn't come.

My clothes were uncomfortable, for one thing. Men actually wore these uncomfortable costumes all over the place, but I didn't see how. And the truth was, I liked Beth. She had one of those smiles that made wrinkles come out from the corners of her eyes. I guess I didn't like lying or doing what I was supposed to do to someone who had a smile like that.

"Good," she said. "You see, your father and I love each other, but I recognize you and your father have a special relationship."

"That's true," I said. *Special* was one word for it. He had left me when I was a baby because it was too hard not to leave me.

I realized that I'd hoped my birth father would have a good reason for why he left me behind. I don't know. Something like we got separated in a storm at sea and my parents left me with their faithful servant, Roderick, and that servant turned out to be less than faithful and sold me to a baby merchant who happened to have connections in Iowa.

Or maybe they were secret agents who had been involved in a Cold War mission and were forced to go live in Russia for a while to save the United States from total annihilation. They left me behind because it was too dangerous to risk their precious child. When they got back, I was already six and living with my new family. They decided, after a lot of struggle, that I was too old to take away from my Iowa parents. Their hearts were broken, but they did what was best for me.

Anyway, I used to make things like this up. But I knew better. Really, I always expected the explanation Dean had given. I wasn't surprised.

I started for the door. I wanted to get out of there.

"I want to get to know you," she said, following. "I want to know everything I can about you. Not now, of course, but later, on our own. I want us to be close if we can. I do love your father."

I had a hard time looking in the general direction of her eyes. I had a hard time not running away.

"Maybe you just think you love him," I said. "People think that stuff all the time. Then, bam, one day they don't."

"I know you're thinking of your mother," she said. "That poor woman."

"What do you mean?"

"Her mental illness," she said, looking pained.

She took my hand. I let her take it.

"Dean said that?"

"He told me," she said, and I saw those wrinkles around her eyes. They weren't as pronounced as when she laughed. "Perhaps he shouldn't have, but he told me she's in that place in the hill country, that private hospital."

"Right, a private hospital," I said, my mind going in all different directions.

"I don't want to have any secrets from you," she said. "I know all about what happened. The hospitals. The doctors."

It sounded like one of Dean's stories to get sympathy, but somehow the tenderness in her voice and the way she held my hand made it real. And I just couldn't do it. I couldn't use her the way Dean wanted. It was wrong.

"If I tell you something," I said, "you promise not to let Dean know I told you? Just not tonight, I mean."

"What do you want to tell me?"

"You have to promise," I said.

She frowned. That's when I saw that she had known all along, although she didn't know she knew, or at least she wouldn't admit it. People did that to themselves all the time.

"You are Dean's son," she said, almost but not quite a question.

"The promise?" I said.

"I'm not going to like this, am I?"

She didn't need an answer, and I didn't give her one.

"I promise, then," she said.

"I'm his son, but I only met him today." Then I told her the rest of it, including what Dean planned to do with her hundred thousand dollars.

I'll say this for her, she didn't blink once. She didn't swoon. She didn't cry. She didn't interrupt. She took her time before she said anything.

"I've been very foolish."

"It's just this is what he does for a living. He's good at it. He likes you. He told me that. But he needs money."

"If he had just asked—"

"He's too proud."

"Proud? But to do this—"

"He doesn't know any better," I said. I realized this was true. He couldn't see beyond what he needed and the easiest way to get what he needed. Dean was lazy in a couple of ways. Too lazy not to use his charm to steal. Too lazy to see how he hurt people.

Christ, I thought, I sound like my father.

Beth still had my hand, and now she gripped it a little tighter than I would have liked. "I'll keep my end of the bargain."

She hugged me then. She looked like she'd fallen down some stairs. I felt bad for her, but I felt bad for me, too. Dean was going to hate me for this. I had just found him, and now I was going to lose him.

Beth and I returned to the party. Not long after that Beth disappeared, and her sister came around and told guests Beth was having one of her migraines.

Dean and I were standing in a group of people listening to a very old man tell an Indian legend. It was kind of interesting. It was the ultimate in rich people entertainment, I guess. They hired this old Indian guy to tell these myths, and if you wanted to, you could listen to one.

I guess this was what happened when you had too much money. You had to find ridiculous ways to spend it.

Dean got all crazy when the sister told him about the headache. He pulled me along and tried to go upstairs, but a security guard blocked his way. Dean made a big scene by calling the sister over, but the sister said the doctor was upstairs with Beth.

"She said she'd call you tomorrow."

Dean told the sister if she was trying to keep him from Beth, it wasn't going to work.

"Her words," the sister said, but she seemed pretty happy she had the chance to say them to Dean.

Dean stormed out of the house, and I had to follow in his wake. What was new? He slammed his open hand on the hood of his car. I couldn't see in the dark, but I thought he probably made a pretty good dent in it.

"Something is going on," he said as we got in the car. "I can smell it. I can smell these things."

He burned rubber leaving the driveway, but then, it seemed to me he burned rubber leaving about everyplace.

"My mother?" I said.

"Your mother," he said.

I got the answer I wanted. I just wondered if it was the truth.

# Venusian **Blue Women** and a Guitar Made of Light

When we got back to the house, Claire wasn't all that happy to see us. She asked me why I was wearing a suit, and I said Dean made me go to a dumb party. That didn't go over well. She didn't like being left out of a party situation.

"It was work," Dean said. "Alan was helping with a little thing I've got going."

"I got off early because I wanted to go out with you and your son, and you were off at some party." Her voice was somewhere between a whine and a threat.

"Really, honey, it was work."

I left them to argue and went to the bedroom to change into my old clothes. I got changed pretty fast. They argued the whole time. Then Claire said, loud enough for me to hear, that she wasn't going to be my mom, and Dean had better rethink his priorities.

If she thought I was ever going to consider her as a mom, she was deluded. She was right about one thing, though. Dean was going to have to do some rethinking pretty soon.

When I came into the room, Claire shook a cigarette from a pack and snapped a match out of a book of matches and lit the cigarette. She stared at Dean but spoke to me.

"Someone called for you," she said.

My first crazy thought was that my mom or dad had somehow found me.

"Who?"

"Andy someone. He's at Brackenridge Hospital. A friend of yours got hurt."

"A friend?"

"Elvis somebody."

"I didn't know you knew anybody in town," Dean said. It sounded sort of funny, like he thought he knew everything about me when he didn't know hardly anything.

"He's a guy I met on the way down. I have to go to the hospital."

"You don't know Austin. I'd better take you."

Dean almost sounded like a dad, but I told him I'd made it all the way from Iowa, and I thought I could find a hospital. He gave me directions.

"We might be out when you get back," Claire said. "I'll leave a key in the mailbox."

"Where we going, darlin'?" Dean asked.

I didn't wait for an answer. When I pulled out, I made the tires squeal. I did it without thinking.

**E**lvis's eyes were swollen almost completely shut. His face was lumpy with colored bruises in various shades of blue and purple. The doctors had him hooked up to machines.

Andy stood by the bed looking down at him with mournful eyes. Cookie sat up very straight in a chair by the window.

"What happened to him?" I said, moving up next to Andy.

Andy reached over and squeezed my hand. "We don't know for sure."

"We know," Cookie said.

"Not for sure."

"Don't be absurd." Cookie smiled slightly. "The motel manager told us that Elvis had been robbed and beat up."

"By who?" I said, though I already knew the answer.

"Don't pretend to be stupid. You aren't stupid. The girl and her giant husband."

"The manager said a woman and a man," Andy said stubbornly. "We don't know it was Charley."

Cookie was all eager to talk. "Oh, please. He said the man was a giant and the woman very pretty. He saw them drive off. She robbed Elvis and left him for dead."

I imagined Charley on the back of the giant's brand-new, shiny Harley bought with Elvis's money. That was something I didn't like seeing, and to get it out of my head, I asked Andy about his visit with his wife.

"We had us a nice talk. She's married to a good man, owns his own business. She's going to set up a meeting between me and the kids. I'm going to finally see them."

Andy asked me about Dean. I was tempted to tell him about this guy who read Tolstoy and fought advertisers, but something stopped me. I didn't make up anything. I left some things out, but I didn't make up one thing.

At nine they were going to kick us out, but the nurse asked if I was Elvis's son and I said yes (I was getting fathers left and right on this trip), and she let me stay a little longer.

About twenty minutes after they all left, Elvis opened his eyes. Opened wasn't exactly accurate because they were so swollen it was more like his pupils peeked out from folds of skin.

"That you, Alan?" he said.

I stepped closer and put my hand on the metal railing attached to the bed. "It's me."

"I don't feel so good."

"You don't look so good," I said.

He groaned. "Charley's gone?"

He knew the answer. "She's gone."

"It was the giant came and took her and my money."

"How'd he find you?"

"Charley got scared. Told him where we were, I guess. I know she let him in the room."

Thinking of her doing that after Elvis had helped her get away from the giant made me mad. I yanked on the rail without thinking. Elvis groaned even louder than before.

"Sorry," I said.

He took a deep breath. He tried his half smile but didn't get very far. "She did try to talk him out of beating me up. At least I can say that much."

"She didn't do a very good job."

Elvis reached down to the plastic box attached to the bed-frame and pushed a little button that raised the top half of the bed.

"He said he owed me a little something. She tried to get between us, and he tossed her off like she was a kitten."

"What about that karate stuff you did last time?"

"He had a gun. I thought he was going to kill me, but he just hit me with it. Last thing I remember seeing was Charley on the floor, over in the corner, cowering like a frightened little animal. She didn't look like herself."

I almost yanked on the rail again, but I caught myself. "You should call the cops."

"She's got herself a hard row to plow. I guess I won't make it any harder."

He looked like it hurt him just to move his mouth, just to keep his eyes open.

"You ought to do something. Look what she did to you."

He raised his hand like a traffic cop stopping traffic. "It don't matter, Alan." Then he sighed and lowered his hand. "You ever heard of a guy named Harrison?"

"I don't think so."

"He was a man who looked just like me and was named after a president of the United States who was supposed to be a distant relative of his, William Henry Harrison. Ever hear of President Harrison?"

I admitted I hadn't.

"No one remembers him. There was bad weather during his inauguration, and he stood out in it giving a long speech, caught pneumonia, and died not long after. Funny way to die, ain't it?"

"I guess."

"When I was Harrison, my wives all left me. I don't seem to be good with the ladies."

"When you were Harrison? What do you mean, when you were Harrison?"

"Not the president, of course. The guy named after the president, Harrison Wayne."

"I heard you sing. I saw your birth certificate. You're Elvis Aron Presley." I knew I sounded a little crazy, but the truth was, I wanted him to be Elvis.

The left side of his mouth made a sad smile. "Let me tell you about Harrison. He was rich. His daddy left him a ton of money, which he spent on all kinds of senseless things like houses and cars and drugs and alcohol. No one seemed to mind that. But then he decided one day, after three wives, to start giving his money away to people who didn't have much of their own. That was when they said he was crazy. His family tried to have him put away. So what he did, he disappeared."

"You were really this Harrison guy?"

"Harrison," he said tiredly. "Poor Harrison."

"He doesn't sound so poor to me," I said, kind of mad.

"The things people think are crazy. Giving money to the poor, being the great Elvis. They can't stand someone who will shake things up."

He mumbled this last sentence and lay back and closed his eyes. I thought he was asleep, but after about half a minute he looked up at me and said he was thirsty.

A plastic cup and pitcher were on a tray on the dresser. I filled the cup with water. His hand was shaking too much to hold it, so I poured little sips between his bruised lips.

"You know what I told you about aliens not mating with earthwomen?"

"You said it wasn't possible."

"Wasn't true."

I saw where this was going, and I didn't like it. I didn't like it one bit. "Do you even know what's true? Do you have any idea?"

"You humans are an untrusting lot, aren't you?" His voice sounded different.

I looked at him again. I was suspicious that he was acting, but maybe he really didn't know what was true. Maybe he didn't have any idea.

"What's your name now?" I said, trying to sound casual, like I'd forgotten it or something.

"I can't tell you that. We have rules. Let's just say you couldn't pronounce my name. I've been exploring this galaxy for centuries, and now I'm here on your beautiful planet. That's all I can say." He raised his eyebrows, and his poor, battered face seemed mischievous. "Come with me, Alan. For you I'd make an exception to our rule about not taking visitors along on our travels. I know a great bar on the other side of Venus. Women as blue as midnight and sweet as Georgia peaches. You like to travel, right?"

I imagined Elvis sitting at the bar with steamy drinks and blue Venusian women hanging on him. Someone would throw him a guitar made of light, and he would launch into a song.

I was about to tell him I'd have to pass, but before I could, he slipped off into sleep. He began to snore lightly.

I put my hand on his arm. I guessed we were alike in one way. Neither of us had a clear idea of who we were. I leaned over and whispered in his ear. I knew I risked sounding like a character in a book my mom would read, so I kept my voice nice and low. "I hope you do make it to a bar on the other side of Venus, Elvis. You deserve a sweet, blue lady."

Andy and Cookie were waiting for me in the lobby. We left the hospital together.

"I think he's going to be all right," I said.

"That's good to hear," Andy said. "That's fine. Cook and I are going to stick around a while, so we'll check in on him."

"I have no intention of becoming someone's nursemaid," Cookie said.

Andy ignored him and looked at me. "You gonna be moving on, Alan?"

"Tonight or tomorrow."

"You should go home where you belong," Cook said.

I thought he might be right, but I sure wouldn't tell him that. We said good-bye, and Andy teared up a little. He was a big blubbery man, but you had to kind of love a guy like that. I guess that's why I said it before I walked off. "It was a pleasure traveling with you, Andy."

He brightened right up with one of his marching band smiles. "The pleasure was all mine, Alan. All mine."

# They Teach You About **William Henry Harrison?**

I went to a Denny's and ordered pie and ice cream and milk. I thought about going back to Dean's, but when the waitress came around again to pick up my empty plate and glass, I ordered some pancakes and coffee and settled in. I decided I was just going to spend the night in the corner booth at Denny's.

It seemed to me it was time to do something, but I didn't know what. Maybe I could go back to Iowa. For the first time since I'd left, I had this idea that maybe I could go back. Maybe it was possible. I didn't think Dean and I were going to the tropics. I liked him, but I had a feeling I couldn't drive as crazy as Dean did without crashing. Anyway, a part of me was a little too—I hated to think it—practical. I didn't want to do the things Dean had to do in order to live the way he lived.

The waitress set my pancakes and my cup of coffee in front of me.

"Guess you're hungry." She had a nice smile.

"A little."

"That all you need?"

I almost told her it wasn't. I needed a lot of things. I didn't know how to get them, though.

"Are you all right?"

I thought about this. I really did. "I've been better, but I'm okay."

She didn't look too convinced, and I wasn't too convinced myself.

It was a long night in the Denny's. A lot of people came in around two-thirty: mostly young or at least not too old, mostly drunk. Every girl, every single one that came in, was pretty. It was almost like a dream that way. Dean would have been disappointed in me because I didn't go on over and introduce myself and try to get the girls' phone numbers.

The thing was, I didn't feel like it. I wasn't Mr. Social, and I never would be. I could think of a lot of things I wasn't. I wasn't Mr. Con; I wasn't Mr. Fix-it; I wasn't Mr. Dealer; I wasn't Mr. Cool; I wasn't Mr. Romance. You know, it didn't do much good, though. What I wanted to do was think of what I was.

One thing I kept turning over in my mind was what Beth had said about my mother being in a mental hospital.

I drank way too much coffee because the waitress kept coming around and refilling my cup. She wasn't a whole lot older than me. Maybe twenty or so. The coffee made me talkative.

"You go to college?" I asked.

"Yep."

"You probably always knew you wanted to go to college."

"Nope," she said, filling my cup one more time. "I wanted to be a ballet dancer until I was fifteen and had a growth spurt. Then I had to go to plan B. How about you?"

"I don't know," I said.

She shrugged. "Not for everyone."

"No."

I could go to Con Man College, but somehow I thought I would flunk out. So there I was. Still thinking about what I didn't want to be and what I wasn't.

"On the other hand," she said, "you don't look like you'd be happy working at a 7-Eleven."

"You like it?"

"College?" she said. "It's okay. It's not easy for me."

"They teach you about William Henry Harrison?"

She shook her head, so I told her about how this guy became president and gave this long speech in a storm and died of pneumonia not long after.

"Bummer," she said.

I didn't have any other interesting facts to share, but oddly enough, she didn't run off.

"Can I ask you a question?"

I couldn't really say no. I nodded.

"You a runaway?"

"I left if that's what you mean. I didn't exactly plan it."

"You think most runaways do?"

She had a point.

After her shift was over, she sat down and talked to me for about an hour. She didn't get all preachy or anything. She just told me what a tough time she'd had in school and with her mother, who was a single mom.

She got me to talk some. She pointed out a few things. Like maybe the reason things got out of control wasn't just one thing but a lot of things, and some of them went way back. Hard to untangle. Hard to understand. But not impossible.

I don't know. If somebody had said these things to me a few weeks ago, I probably wouldn't have listened. It was like sometimes you couldn't hear things until you were ready to hear them.

But also it was just kind of fascinating that this pretty college girl was taking the time to talk to me after her shift was over. There were a lot of unkind and nasty people in the world, but there were some who would take the time to talk to a stranger just because they thought he needed it.

You could say a lot of things against the world, but it was sort of hard to overlook a thing like that.

# Coming **Unstuck** in Time

I called Dean at about seven o'clock in the morning.

"Where the hell are you?" he said. "No, forget that. Why in the hell are you calling me now? What time is it?"

"Denny's, seven o'clock," I said, "and I want you to tell me where my mother is."

"Jesus Christ, kid."

"She's here, isn't she? In Austin, I mean. You told Beth. Unless that was a lie, too."

"No, that wasn't a lie."

"In a mental hospital?"

Some old lady walking to the rest room gave me a disapproving look. I glared back at her.

"In a care facility. A very nice one."

"Are you going to tell me where or not? I can find her on my own if I have to."

Silence. For a moment I thought he'd hung up on me.

"She's not herself, Alan. She's not all here. Her mind isn't, anyway. She doesn't even know who I am sometimes. She won't remember you."

"Maybe not, but I have to see her."

He made one of those long theatrical sighs. "You won't let it go?"

"I can't."

"No, I suppose not," he said. "You wouldn't let any of this go, which is why you're here in the first place. You ran away from your folks in Iowa, didn't you?"

"Things weren't going too well."

"Your folks didn't do any bad things to you, did they?"

"It was me. I was the problem."

"Just you, huh?"

"Everything sort of got out of hand."

"Things have a way of doing that," he said.

"Yeah. Well, maybe I let them some."

He paused like he was thinking something over. Then he said, "She's still the most precious thing in my life, Alan. I wouldn't want her hurt."

"I just need to see she's real," I said, and it wasn't until I'd said this I knew it was true. Funny how it worked that way sometimes. Words came out, and you didn't know where they came from, but they were absolutely right just by themselves.

"Okay," he said. "It's called River Ranch. About thirty miles out of town."

He gave me directions.

"Thanks, Dean."

"Be easy on her, Alan. Be gentle."

I waited another hour and made the drive.

River Ranch was in the hill country to the west of Austin. It looked like a pretty nice place for crazy people. It looked like a pretty nice place even if you weren't crazy.

The grounds were green pastures, and there was a rose garden right in front of the main house. Off to one side was a stream. The house looked like one of those old mansions from *Gone with the Wind.*

I parked my car in the parking lot and went in. The lobby had cheerful paintings on the walls, big comfortable leather chairs, and black-and-white tile floors. Even my mom couldn't have found something that needed cleaning.

The front desk looked like one in a fancy hotel. An old woman stood behind it and gave me the eye as I walked across the lobby.

"I'm looking for Kate Dalton," I said.

"Are you related?"

"I'm her son."

"Just a moment," the woman said. She went back to a filing cabinet behind the desk and pulled out a file. She fumbled with reading glasses on a chain around her neck.

Before she even started reading, I said, "I'm not in there, but I'm her son."

She looked up over the top of her glasses the way some people do. "We have very strict policies. Only family may visit except by special written permission."

"Call Dean. He'll tell you. She's my mother."

The woman stared at me, and I stared right back. She must have seen how desperate I looked. She frowned and sighed one of those deep adult sighs. "Room 21. She's awake. She always rises early. Don't you cause me any trouble, young man."

That was a long hallway down to the room. The place didn't look at all like a hospital. It just looked like a big house. Pictures on the wall. Nice wood floors. It was a little too clean and neat for my tastes, but at least it wasn't what I was picturing on the drive out, which was something from *One Flew Over the Cuckoo's Nest*. People in pajamas and robes and drool coming out of mouths and stuff like that. I saw one other patient, a man in a suit, who passed by me in the hallway.

"Good day," he said.

I said good day back.

I knocked on the door to Room 21, which was open enough that light came out from it into the hall.

"Come in," she said.

She had a strong Texas accent. I wondered why she didn't ask who was there. Just "Come in."

I went in.

It was a big room. It was divided up so that one side was a bedroom: a bed, a dresser, a night table, a lamp. There was no mirror. The other side of the room had a table and two chairs in front of a window and a reading chair and another lamp in the corner. She was sitting in a window chair but got right up and came over to me and put the palm of her hand on my cheek; her hand was scratchy, but I didn't care.

"It's a pleasure meeting you. Thank you for stopping by."

I saw some of myself in Dean, but I saw a lot more of myself in her. It was scary, and it wasn't, too.

I tried to smile. My throat felt dry. You could have thrown a little sand in that throat and called it a desert.

"It's very peaceful here, isn't it?" she said.

She slipped her arm over mine and guided me to a chair by the window and told me to please sit down. It was peaceful. From the window you saw the river off in the distance and a well-kept field down to the river. Off to one side was a garden with lots of colorful flowers. A few deer ate something close to the garden. It looked like a little chunk of paradise, all right. The only problem was, you had to be crazy to have her view.

"Do you like it here?" I asked.

She sat down in the other chair. She was thin and wore a long flowing dress. Her eyes were very dark and very big. "Oh yes. I'm not good in places that aren't peaceful."

"How long have you been here?"

"I couldn't say. I've been here forever and not at all."

That seemed a little vague, but I just nodded like it made perfect sense.

The fingers of her right hand tapped on the arm of the chair. Not randomly. It was like she had some song playing in her mind.

"I read this book. People become unstuck. In time. Billy Pilgrim became unstuck. I became unstuck. Billy Pilgrim and me."

She seemed to be looking over my shoulder, and I had an idea maybe this Billy Pilgrim was another patient and had stepped into the room. I looked, but no one was there.

She smiled. "In the book, silly. He's in the book. I read about him being unstuck, and I knew I was unstuck, too. I knew all about falling from one moment to another without any control. I might write my own book someday."

I thought about this, how a person might fall from one moment to another. "You mean like a time traveler?"

"I'm not crazy, you know. I just can't keep myself in one time. That's not being crazy, is it? Anyone would become confused moving around in time like I do."

"I imagine they would." I was a little disappointed. I mean, I'd known she was in a mental hospital, but I guess some part of me had hoped there was a mistake.

She seemed distracted by something outside on the lawn. I couldn't see anything. She just kept staring. I tried to think of what to do or say. A minute passed. She turned toward me. Her voice was excited. "Mother was shouting. She was shouting from the bedroom."

The way she looked scared me a little. It was like she was on a high ledge looking down. I stayed perfectly still.

She leaned toward me and whispered, "I never could like Mother. Love but not like. It was always hard between us."

I could see that she had once been very beautiful. She still was, but something was missing in her, too. I must have been staring because she sat back. "I've been gone, haven't I?"

"Yes," I said.

"Where was I? I can never remember clearly. Like a dream. It's always like a dream. Have I ruined our conversation?"

Her right hand tapped differently on the chair arm. Fast and unrhythmic, like she'd lost track of the song in her head.

"You haven't ruined anything."

Her smile came slow to her face; it was a girlish smile. "That's really very kind. I can see that you're a kind boy."

I could have told her some things, but I didn't. "You were only gone a second."

Her right hand tapped less frantically. We sat in silence for a little while, and finally the tapping seemed more like before.

"What was I saying?" she asked.

"You were telling me about being unstuck in time."

"I was? Well, yes, it confuses me. I lose track of things. I wish I wouldn't lose track."

"It's like you said, who wouldn't get confused?"

"You're a good boy. Would you like a cookie?"

Before I could answer, she got up and went over to a closet.

It was sort of like when I saw Dean with that baseball bat. Moms asked their sons if they wanted cookies. Of course, I was a little old for that.

She came back with a tin box and sat next to me, balancing it on her lap while she pried off the lid. She held the box under my chin and shook it. I took a cookie. What else was I going to do? I took a bite. Chocolate chip. Pretty good. One thing was sure, the cookies on this trip were excellent.

"Who sent you?" she said, trying to sound offhand but watching me closely.

"I'm a friend of Dean's." The words kind of caught in my throat. They came out crumpled. She didn't seem to notice.

"Dean," she said. "Why didn't you say so? Oh, you should have seen Dean when I first met him. We were twenty, I think. He was beautiful."

She laughed in a pleasant way, not at all the movie version of the typical crazy person's laugh. "Another cookie?"

I said no thanks, and she handed me one like I'd said yes.

"Dean and I fell in love very quickly." She sighed and took a bite of a cookie. "You only fall in love like that once. Am I talking crazy?"

"No."

"Black is white. Red is night. Sunlight. Sunlight. How about now?"

"That sounded kind of crazy to me," I had to admit.

She nodded. "Just testing. Now, what was I saying?"

"About you and Dean."

"It was always the same things that broke us up. Always the same."

"What kind of things?"

"I like you, Alan. You're curious. Curiosity is good. It did not kill the cat. You know what killed the cat?"

"You know my name?"

"I remembered when you said Dean sent you."

"You know who I am?"

"Dean called a few minutes before you arrived. You look just like my brother did at your age. I should have remembered before."

I felt my face flush a little. "I just wanted to meet you."

"Your parents, are they good people?"

"Yes."

They were, I guess. They could have told me to hit the road at any time. I'd given them enough reasons. They could have done a lot of things to me that they didn't.

"What was I going to tell you?"

"The things that broke you and Dean up."

"No, that wasn't it."

"What killed the cat?" I said without thinking.

"Not curiosity. Not Dean. Oh, I could blame some people, my mother for one, but no, that wouldn't be right, either. Maybe there was nothing that could be done. The cat just died. But you should know that Dean stayed with me until you were born. Then we did the only thing two people like us could do. We gave you up."

"You named me, though. The name was on the adoption paper."

"After my father."

"After your father." It was a small fact, but it was like I had a history in a way I hadn't before. I was named after someone.

She frowned. "This must be a letdown. A crazy woman for your mother."

"I'm happy I came," I said.

When her dark brown eyes looked into mine this time, I saw my own eyes. And her expression was like mine sometimes. And her hair. Curly like mine. I saw lots of similarities. It was hard to say exactly how the world changed in that moment, but it did. I felt connected to her, and somehow I felt more connected to myself. I don't know. Everything in my life seemed a little closer, even my Iowa parents, even my life back in Iowa.

"You'll come to see me again?" she said.

"Sure I will. I'll call."

"Write," she said. "I love to get letters, and Dean never writes. Poor Dean. Don't be too hard on him. He pays a lot of money to keep me here."

"I know."

"I'm slipping. I'm falling. Forgive me if I get confused about who you are next time, curious Alan."

"I forgive you," I said.

She gazed out the window again. Then she looked at me, but I could tell she wasn't really seeing me.

"This is the first time in my life I've seen the Grateful Dead. What a trip. Rainbow people everywhere. Rainbow people everywhere you look."

I left her sitting by the window.

# You Have a **Live Girlfriend** the Next Time We Talk

I drove to Dean's expecting to get beat up because by then he would have talked to Beth. He opened the door. First thing I saw was his suitcase by the sofa.

"There he is. King of the road," he said. Then he smiled in that same sad way he had out at the lake when he'd first told me about Kate. "How was she?"

"She was fine," I said. "At the end she went off to a Grateful Dead concert. Her first Grateful Dead concert."

He smiled. "San Francisco. We were there together. Yeah, that was a good time."

"Where are you going?"

"Hawaii. Thanks to you."

"I'm sorry."

He shrugged. "I should have known better. Just like your mother. Soft heart."

I didn't have any soft heart. I was about to tell him this, but he picked up the suitcase and hugged me and I couldn't say anything.

"I thought you'd be mad," I said when I could.

"I was mad as hell. But what are you going to do? What's done is done. I'm going to Hawaii before Sally catches up with me. Want to come along? I still think, with a little guidance, you could be a decent con man."

"I better go home," I said.

"Thought you might say that. Well, I'm off, then. No time to hang around."

I walked out the door with him.

"How will I find you?" I said.

"I'll find you. And you know where Kate is."

"Yeah. You could send me a postcard."

"I'm no good at writing," he said.

He threw the suitcase in his car and hopped in.

"Don't disappoint me, now," he said, starting the car. "You have a live girlfriend the next time we talk."

He squealed his tires when he drove off.

I drove downtown to Sixth Street. I parked the car and walked past bars and restaurants. This guy on the street, a street person sitting on a curb, asked me if I knew who he was. He wore a helmet and army fatigues, and I should have just ignored him, but I didn't. I shrugged.

"I'm Jesus Christ the Savior. I died for your sins. I can't even afford a cup of coffee. Don't you think you could spare a couple of cents for the Savior? Don't you think that's the least you can do?"

"Do you know who I am?" I said.

He looked me over carefully.

"Barbra Streisand?"

"Simon the Iowan," I said. "Alan the Texan."

"Never heard of you. How about that change?"

I reached in my pocket and gave him what I had. He made a bugle sound by blowing through his closed hand.

He turned to me.

"May I be with you," he said.

I walked into a restaurant called Paradise and went to the back where the phones were and dialed my parents' number. My dad answered.

I couldn't say anything at first. He said hello a second time, his voice a little tight. He never was very patient on the phone.

"Dad?"

"Simon?"

"It's me." I guess I wasn't too sure what that meant, but I had a better idea now.

"Are you all right?"

"I think so," I said. "Yeah, I'm okay."

"Don't hang up."

"I won't."

"Where are you?"

"I'm in Texas. I'm sorry. I'm sorry for all this."

"But you're all right."

"Yeah, I'm okay. Is it okay if I come home?"

"I'll come and get you. I—Jesus, Simon, we've been going crazy here."

"I'm sorry I'm such a screwup, I—"

"Don't say that. You aren't a screwup. You screw up, but you aren't a screwup. We love you, son. You better talk to your mother. You don't move, okay? I'm going to come and get you."

"Okay, Dad."

"Here's your mom."

Just as my mom said my name, a recorded voice said I needed to put more money in the pay phone or I would be disconnected. My mom told me to hang up and she would call right back, and if I didn't pick up the phone, I was going to be in more trouble than I could imagine. I don't know why, but I kind of liked hearing this.

I picked up the phone when it rang.

My mom and I talked for close to an hour. I didn't tell her about finding Dean and Kate, though. I wasn't sure what I was going to do about that yet. I just knew I wasn't going to tell them right away.

Also, there would be the problem of Martin waiting for me when I got back. I was going to have to pay him and do some serious ass-kissing to keep from bodily injury. I thought I could do that, though.

I guess I knew there were things I couldn't do much about. Trinity wasn't going to love me. The world wasn't going to straighten up and ban advertising. Kate wasn't going to stop being crazy. My dad wasn't going to change his mind and think keeping a nice yard, fixing broken appliances, and building houses were anything less than the highest calling of man. I couldn't do much about these things, but I could do something about how I took these things.

That was one way I hadn't looked at it before, and I should have. It was kind of like my two grandmothers, like how they were different. They both had bad husbands—alcoholics who died suddenly. They both raised their kids on their own. They both spent many years working hard and boring jobs that paid them just enough to get by. But my dad's mom could make me happy just by looking at her. She liked to run around the house barefooted, and she laughed all the time and enjoyed just about everything she did. My mom's mom was the opposite. She hardly left her house and all she did was watch TV, and most of the time she looked like she had just eaten something that tasted very, very sour. But you looked at the facts of their lives, and they were about the same.

**M**y dad and mom flew down to get me the next day. My dad didn't even yell at me about the dents in his car when he saw them. We took the long way back to Iowa through Colorado, and I even had a pretty good time with them. I mean, it was a little embarrassing when my mom read one of her romance novels at the pool of a motel. And my dad yelled at me when I burned rubber pulling out of a Quality Inn. Also, my dad irritated me when he talked about—well, about a lot of things. Still, we had a pretty good time. We weren't going to give up on one another. That much had been decided without us really talking about it.

**"Y**ou ever feel like you're in two places at once?" I asked my dad as we pulled into Mansfield city limits.

My mom was asleep in the backseat. My dad frowned at me. I thought he was about to tell me I should concentrate on being in just one place. Being in one place was hard enough, especially for someone like me.

"Tell you what, Simon," he said. "You're a smart kid. You can probably do a lot of things I can't. But that doesn't mean I want to hear about them all."

"That means no, I guess."

"You got that right, kiddo. Think you can pull into our drive without squealing the tires?"

"I think I can do that," I said.

# Ac**know**ledgments

Thanks to my editor, Debby Vetter, for her insight and skill, to my agent Ronnie Herman, to my publisher Marc Aronson, to Cynthia Leitich Smith for early encouragement and advice, and most of all to my wife, Frances Hill, for unfailing support and for being my best friend.